PENGUIN CLASSICS

Maigret and the Old L

'I love reading Simenon. He makes me think of Chekhov'
– William Faulkner

'A truly wonderful writer . . . marvellously readable – lucid, simple, absolutely in tune with the world he creates'
– Muriel Spark

'Few writers have ever conveyed with such a sure touch, the bleakness of human life' – A. N. Wilson

'One of the greatest writers of the twentieth century . . . Simenon was unequalled at making us look inside, though the ability was masked by his brilliance at absorbing us obsessively in his stories' – *Guardian*

'A novelist who entered his fictional world as if he were part of it' – Peter Ackroyd

'The greatest of all, the most genuine novelist we have had in literature' – André Gide

'Superb . . . The most addictive of writers . . . A unique teller of tales' – *Observer*

'The mysteries of the human personality are revealed in all their disconcerting complexity' – Anita Brookner

'A writer who, more than any other crime novelist, combined a high literary reputation with popular appeal' – P. D. James

'A supreme writer . . . Unforgettable vividness' – *Independent*

'Compelling, remorseless, brilliant' – John Gray

'Extraordinary masterpieces of the twentieth century'
– John Banville

ABOUT THE AUTHOR

Georges Simenon was born on 12 February 1903 in Liège, Belgium, and died in 1989 in Lausanne, Switzerland, where he had lived for the latter part of his life. Between 1931 and 1972 he published seventy-five novels and twenty-eight short stories featuring Inspector Maigret.

Simenon always resisted identifying himself with his famous literary character, but acknowledged that they shared an important characteristic:

> My motto, to the extent that I have one, has been noted often enough, and I've always conformed to it. It's the one I've given to old Maigret, who resembles me in certain points . . . 'understand and judge not'.

Penguin is publishing the entire series of Maigret novels.

GEORGES SIMENON

Maigret and the Old Lady

Translated by ROS SCHWARTZ

PENGUIN BOOKS

PENGUIN CLASSICS

UK | USA | Canada | Ireland | Australia
India | New Zealand | South Africa

Penguin Books is part of the Penguin Random House group of companies whose addresses can be found at global.penguinrandomhouse.com.

First published in French as *Maigret et la vieille dame* by Presses de la Cité 1950
This translation first published 2016
002

Typeset in Dante MT Std by Palimpsest Book Production Ltd, Falkirk, Stirlingshire
Printed in Great Britain by Clays Ltd, St Ives plc

ISBN: 978–0–241–20682–9

www.greenpenguin.co.uk

Contents

1. *The Lady of La Bicoque*

He alighted from the Paris–Le Havre train at the bleak little station of Bréauté-Beuzeville. He'd had to get up at five o'clock and, unable to find a taxi, had taken the first Métro to Gare Saint-Lazare. Now he was waiting for his connection.

'The train to Étretat, please?'

Although the time was past eight o'clock and it had been broad daylight for ages, it felt like dawn here because of the drizzle and the damp cold.

There was no restaurant in the station, no refreshment room, only a sort of tavern on the opposite side of the road, where the old carts belonging to the livestock traders were stationed.

'Étretat? You've got plenty of time. Your train's over there.'

The man pointed at the carriages without a locomotive waiting in a siding. They were old-style carriages, painted a green that was rarely seen nowadays. Behind the windows sat a few rigid passengers who looked as if they'd been waiting since the previous day. There was something unreal about the train. It was more like a toy, or a child's drawing.

A family – Parisians, of course! – ran towards the engineless train until they were out of breath, goodness knows why, picking their way over the rails, the three children carrying shrimping nets.

That was what triggered the memory. For a moment Maigret was ageless and, even though they were at least twenty kilometres from the sea, he had the impression he could smell the salty tang and hear the rhythmic pounding of the waves; he looked up and gazed with a certain awe at the grey clouds that must have drifted in from the sea.

Maigret had been born and spent his childhood far inland, and his image of the seaside had remained unchanged: shrimping nets, a toy train, men in flannel trousers, beach umbrellas, hawkers selling seashells and souvenirs, cafés serving white wine and oysters, and family boarding houses which all had the same smell, one that is peculiar to those family boarding houses where, after a few days, Madame Maigret felt so miserable doing nothing with her hands that she would gladly have offered to help with the washing-up.

He knew, of course, that it was illusory, but the image of a cheery, artificial world where nothing grim could ever happen resurfaced whenever he found himself close to the sea.

During the course of his career he had carried out several investigations on the coast and had seen some real tragedies. And yet, as he drank a Calvados at the bar of the tavern, he was tempted to smile once again at the thought of the old lady named Valentine and her stepson, Besson.

It was September, Wednesday 6 September, and as usual

Maigret hadn't managed to take the time off to go on a summer holiday. At around eleven o'clock the previous day the old clerk had come into his office at Quai des Orfèvres and handed him a visiting card with a black border.

Madame Ferdinand Besson, widow
La Bicoque
Étretat

'Is she specifically asking to see me?'

'She insists on seeing you, even if it's only for a moment. She says she's come all the way from Étretat.'

'What's she like?'

'She's an old lady. A delightful old lady.'

The clerk showed her in and she was indeed the sweetest old lady imaginable, slender and petite, with a delicate pink face and immaculate white hair, so lively and so gracious that she seemed more like an actress playing an elderly marchioness than a real old lady.

'You probably have no idea who I am, detective chief inspector, which makes me all the more grateful to you for being so kind as to see me. I know about you from having read about your fascinating cases for many years. If you come to my home, as I hope you will, I can even show you countless newspaper cuttings.'

'Thank you very much.'

'My name is Valentine Besson, which doubtless means nothing to you, but it may ring a bell when I tell you that my husband, Ferdinand Besson, invented Juva beauty products.'

Maigret was old enough to be familiar with the name Juva. As a boy he had seen it in newspaper advertisements and on billboards, and he thought he remembered his mother using Juva cream on special occasions when she put on her best clothes.

The elderly lady before him was dressed with studied elegance, slightly old-fashioned, and wore a large amount of jewellery.

'Since my husband's death five years ago, I've lived alone in a little house I own in Étretat. Or rather, until last Sunday evening I lived there alone with a maid who'd been with me for several years, a local girl. She died on Sunday night, inspector; she died instead of me in a way, and that is why I've come to request your help.'

She did not sound melodramatic. Her faint smile seemed to be apologizing for speaking of tragic things.

'Don't worry, I'm not mad. I am not even what people call a batty old woman. When I say that Rose – that was my maid's name – died instead of me, I am almost certain I am not mistaken. May I briefly explain?'

'Please do.'

'For at least twenty years I have been in the habit of taking medication at night to help me sleep. It's a fairly bitter medicine, and the taste is disguised by a strong aniseed flavour. I know what I'm talking about because my husband was a pharmacist.

'Last Sunday, before retiring, I prepared my sleeping draught as usual and got into bed. Rose was with me when I wanted to drink it.

'I took a sip and thought it tasted more bitter than usual.

'"I must have put in more than twelve drops, Rose. I shan't have any more," I said.

'"Good night, Madame."

'She took away the glass. Did she try it out of curiosity? Did she finish off the entire glass? It's likely, because the empty glass was found in her room.

'During the night, at around two o'clock in the morning, I was woken by the sound of groaning, because the house isn't very big. I got up and bumped into my daughter, who had also got up.'

'I thought you lived alone with your maid?'

'Sunday was my birthday, the third of September, and my daughter, who was visiting from Paris, stayed the night.

'I don't want to take up too much of your time, inspector. We found Rose lying in bed, dying. My daughter ran to fetch Doctor Jolly, but by the time he arrived Rose was dead, having suffered convulsions.

'The doctor had no hesitation in certifying that she had been poisoned with arsenic.

'Since she wasn't the sort of girl to commit suicide, and since she'd eaten exactly the same food as us, it is fairly obvious that the poison was in the medicine that I was meant to take.'

'Do you have any suspicions as to who might have attempted to kill you?'

'Who on earth could I suspect? Doctor Jolly, who's an old friend and who treated my husband, telephoned the police in Le Havre, and an inspector came straight away on Monday morning.'

'Do you know his name?'

'Inspector Castaing. A dark-haired man with a ruddy complexion.'

'I know him. What did he say?'

'He didn't say anything. He questioned the local people. The body was taken to Le Havre for the autopsy.'

She was interrupted by the telephone ringing. Maigret picked it up. It was the head of the Police Judiciaire.

'Would you come and see me in my office for a moment, Maigret?'

'Right away?'

'If possible.'

He apologized to the elderly lady.

The chief was waiting for him.

'How would you like to spend a few days by the sea?' he asked.

Why did Maigret reply without thinking:

'In Étretat?'

'How do you know?'

'I don't. Tell me about it.'

'I've just received a telephone call from the minister's office. Do you know Charles Besson?'

'Is he also of Juva creams?'

'Not exactly. He's the son. Charles Besson lives in Fécamp and was elected deputy for the Lower Seine region two years ago.'

'And his mother lives in Étretat.'

'Not his mother, his stepmother. She's his father's second wife. What I'm telling you now, mind you, I've only just learned myself over the telephone. Charles

Besson has spoken to the minister to request that you handle a case in Étretat, even though it's not your patch.'

'His stepmother's servant was poisoned on Sunday night.'

'Do you read the Normandy newspapers?'

'No. The old lady is in my office.'

'To ask you to go to Étretat as well?'

'Exactly. She made the journey especially, which suggests that she's unaware of her stepson's involvement.'

'What have you decided?'

'That depends on you, chief.'

That was why, shortly after half past eight on the following Wednesday at Bréauté-Beuzeville, Maigret finally boarded a train so small that it was hard to believe it was real. He leaned out of the window to catch a glimpse of the sea at the first opportunity.

As they approached the sky brightened and, when the train emerged from between the hills covered in pastureland, it was a pale blue wash with just a few light, fluffy clouds.

Maigret had telephoned the Le Havre Flying Squad the previous day to inform Inspector Castaing of his arrival, but there was no sign of him as he alighted. Women in summer frocks and bare-chested children waiting on the platform created a holiday mood. The stationmaster, who seemed to be scrutinizing the passengers anxiously, approached Maigret:

'Would you happen to be Monsieur Maigret by any chance?'

'I would happen to be him, yes.'

'Then I have a message for you.'

He handed him an envelope. Castaing had written:

My apologies for not being there to meet you. I am at Yport, at the funeral. I recommend the Hôtel des Anglais, where I hope to join you for lunch and put you in the picture.

It was only ten o'clock and Maigret, who had brought just a light suitcase, made his way on foot to the hotel, which was close to the beach.

But before going in, and despite his suitcase, he went to look at the sea and at the white cliffs enclosing the pebble beach; there were boys and girls cavorting in the waves, and others playing tennis at the back of the hotel; mothers sat knitting in deck chairs while elderly couples shuffled across the sand.

For years, when he was a schoolboy, he had seen his friends come back from their holidays, tanned, with lots of stories to tell and their pockets full of shells. He had been earning his living for a long time before he too was able to gaze at the sea.

He was a little saddened by the realization that he no longer experienced that little thrill, watching with an indifferent eye the dazzling foam on the waves and the lifeguard with bare, tattooed arms in his boat, which was sometimes obscured from view by a huge wave.

The smell of the hotel was so familiar that he felt a pang and suddenly missed Madame Maigret, because it was always with her that he had inhaled that particular smell.

'Do you intend to stay long?' asked the man behind the desk.

'I have no idea.'

'I'm asking because we shut on the 15th of September and today's already the 6th.'

Everything would be closed and the town would look like an empty stage set – the souvenir shops and patisseries would be shuttered, and the deserted beach would be returned to the sea and to the gulls.

'Do you know Madame Besson?'

'Valentine? Of course I know her. She's a local girl, she was born here. Her father was a fisherman. I didn't know her as a child because I'm younger than her, but I can remember when she was an assistant at the Seuret sisters' patisserie. One of the sisters died but the other one's still alive. She's ninety-two. Her house isn't far from Valentine's, actually; there's a blue fence around the garden. Would you mind filling in your form?'

The manager – the owner perhaps? – read it and studied Maigret with more interest.

'Are you the Maigret from the police? And you've come from Paris specially for this case?'

'Inspector Castaing's staying here, isn't he?'

'Well, since Monday he's been eating most of his meals here, but he goes back to Le Havre every night.'

'I'm expecting him.'

'He's at the funeral, in Yport.'

'I know.'

'Do you think someone really tried to poison Valentine?'

'I haven't had the time to form an opinion.'

'If they did, it can only have been one of the family.'

'Do you mean her daughter?'

'I don't mean anyone in particular. I know nothing. There were a lot of them at La Bicoque last Sunday. And I can't think who, around here, would have it in for Valentine. You have no idea how much good that woman did when she had money, when her husband was alive. She still does and, even though she's not rich, she only thinks about giving to others. It's an ugly business, believe me; Étretat has always been a quiet place. Our policy is to keep to a select clientele, chiefly families, preferably of a certain social class. I could tell you . . .'

Maigret preferred to go for a stroll through the sunny streets. Coming into Place de la Mairie, he saw a sign above a white shop front: 'Pâtisserie Maurin, formerly Pâtisserie Seuret'.

He asked a delivery man the way to La Bicoque, and was shown a path that snaked gently down the hillside dotted with a few houses surrounded by gardens. He stopped at a distance from a house hidden among the greenery, where a wisp of smoke could be seen rising slowly from the chimney against the pale blue of the sky, and by the time he returned to the hotel, Inspector Castaing had arrived; his little black Simca was parked outside the entrance and he himself was waiting at the top of the steps.

'Did you have a good journey, sir? I'm very sorry I wasn't able to come and meet you at the station. I thought it would be a good idea to attend the funeral. If what I hear is true, that's your method too.'

'How did it go?'

They set off along the seafront.

'I don't know. I feel like saying: rather badly. There was something unspoken in the air. The girl's body had been brought from Le Havre this morning, and the parents were waiting at the station in a van that drove them to Yport. It's the Trochu family. You'll hear about them. There are lots of Trochus around here, nearly all of them fishermen. The father caught herring around Fécamp for years, as the two older boys still do. Rose was the eldest daughter. There are two or three others, one of them works in a café in Le Havre.'

Castaing had thick hair and a low forehead, and he pursued his idea as single-mindedly as he would have pushed a plough.

'I've been based at Le Havre for six years now and got to know every corner of the region. In the villages, and especially around the chateaux, you still come across respectful, humble people who speak of "our master". There are others who are tougher, suspicious, sometimes resentful, tetchy. I don't know yet which category the Trochus come under, but this morning the atmosphere around Valentine Besson was distinctly cold, almost menacing.'

'Earlier I was told she was well loved in Étretat.'

'Yport isn't Étretat. And young Rose, as she was called here, is dead.'

'So the old lady was at the funeral?'

'Yes, in the front pew. Some people call her the Chatelaine, possibly because she once had a chateau in the Orne, or in Sologne, I can't recall. Have you met her?'

'She came to Paris to see me.'

'She told me she was going to Paris, but I didn't know that it was to see you. What do you make of her?'

'Nothing for the time being.'

'She was once colossally wealthy. For years she had her Paris mansion in Avenue d'Iéna, her chateau and her yacht, while La Bicoque was just a pied-à-terre.

'She'd come here in a big chauffeur-driven limousine, and another car followed behind with the luggage. She caused a stir on Sundays when she attended mass, sitting in the front row (she still has her pew in the church), and she would hand out fistfuls of money. If someone was in need, people would say: "Go and see Valentine."

'Many still call her by her first name, especially the old folk.

'This morning she arrived in Yport by taxi, alighting with all the airs and graces of her past grandeur. It was as if she were the one conducting the funeral. She brought a huge wreath, which completely dwarfed the others.

'I may be mistaken, but I had the impression that the Trochus were annoyed and were giving her filthy looks. She insisted on shaking the hand of each member of the family and the father held his out reluctantly, refusing to look her in the eye. One of the sons, Henri, the eldest, quite simply turned his back on her.'

'Did Madame Besson's daughter accompany her?'

'She went back to Paris on Monday on the afternoon train. I had no authority to stop her. You must already have realized that I'm out of my depth. But I do think we'll need to question her again.'

'What's she like?'

'Like her mother must have been at her age, in other words at thirty-eight. She looks twenty-five. She's petite and slim, very pretty, with huge eyes that nearly always have an expression of childlike innocence. All the same, on Sunday night a man, who wasn't her husband, slept in her room at La Bicoque.'

'Did she tell you that?'

'No, I found out, but too late to ask her about it. I'll have to tell you all about it in detail. This case is a lot more complicated than it seems, and I've had to write everything down. May I?'

He took from his pocket a stylish red leather-bound notebook which bore little resemblance to the laundress's pad that Maigret normally used.

'We received a call at Le Havre at seven o'clock on Monday morning, and I found a memo on my desk when I arrived at eight. I took the Simca and arrived here just after nine. Charles Besson was getting out of a car just in front of me.'

'Does he live in Fécamp?'

'He has a house, and his family lives there all year round; but since being elected he spends part of his time in Paris, where he has an apartment on Boulevard Raspail. He was here all of last Sunday with his family, in other words his wife and their four children.'

'He's not Valentine's son, is he?'

'Valentine doesn't have any sons, only a daughter, Arlette, the one I told you about and who's married to a Parisian dentist.'

'Was the dentist here too on Sunday?'

'No. Arlette came alone. It was her mother's birthday. Apparently it's a family tradition to visit her on her birthday. When I asked her which train she had taken, she told me the morning train, the same one that you took.

'But she wasn't telling the truth, as you'll see. The first thing I did on Monday, as soon as the body had been taken to Le Havre, was to examine every room in the house. That was some job, because although it's small and charming, the place is full of nooks and crannies, fragile items of furniture and knick-knacks.

'Apart from Valentine's bedroom and the maid's room, both on the first floor, there is only one guest room, on the ground floor, which Arlette was staying in. When I moved the bedside table I found a man's handkerchief, and I had the feeling that the young woman, who was watching me work, suddenly became distraught. She snatched it out of my hands, saying: "I've taken one of my husband's handkerchiefs again!"

'I don't know why, but it was only that evening that I recalled the embroidered monogram, an "H". Arlette had just left. I'd offered to drive her to the station in my car, and I watched her buy her ticket at the window.

'It's stupid, I know, but as I was getting back into the car, I was struck by the fact that she hadn't bought a return ticket when she came. I went back into the waiting room and questioned the ticket collector.

'"That lady arrived on the ten o'clock train on Sunday, didn't she?"

'"What lady?"

'"The one I've just dropped off."

'"Madame Arlette? No, monsieur."

'"She didn't arrive on Sunday?"

'"She may have arrived on Sunday, but not on the train. It was me who collected the tickets and I'd have recognized her."'

Castaing looked at Maigret with some anxiety.

'Are you listening to me?'

'Yes, yes, of course.'

'Perhaps I'm going into unnecessary detail?'

'Not at all. I need to familiarize myself.'

'With what?'

'With everything – the station, Valentine, Arlette, the ticket collector, the Trochus. Only yesterday I knew nothing of all this.'

'When I went back to La Bicoque, I asked Valentine her son-in-law's name. He's called Julien Sudre, so neither of his initials is an "H". Her two stepsons are called Théo and Charles Besson. There's only the gardener who works for her three days a week, whose name is Honoré; but first of all he wasn't there on Sunday, and then I discovered that he only uses large handkerchiefs with a red leaf pattern.

'Not knowing where to begin the investigation, I started questioning the local people, and that was how I found out from the newspaper seller that Arlette had arrived not by train but by car, a flashy green sports car.

'Then it was easy. The owner of the sports car had reserved a room for Sunday night at the hotel I recommended to you.

'He's a certain Hervé Peyrot, who gave his profession

as wine merchant on the hotel registration form. He lives in Paris, Quai des Grands-Augustins.'

'Did he not sleep at the hotel?'

'He stayed in the hotel bar until it closed, just before midnight, after which, instead of going up to his room he set off on foot, saying he wanted to see the sea. According to the night watchman, he didn't come back until two thirty in the morning. I talked to the shoeshine boy and he told me that the soles of Peyrot's shoes had red mud on them.

'On the Tuesday morning I returned to La Bicoque and found footprints in a flower bed beneath the window of Arlette's room.

'What do you make of that?'

'Nothing.'

'As for Théo Besson . . .'

'Was he there too?'

'Not during the night. You understand, don't you, that the two Besson sons are the offspring of a first marriage and that Valentine isn't their mother? I've sketched out the family tree if you're interested.'

'Not now, I'm hungry.'

'In short, Théo Besson, who's forty-eight and unmarried, has been on holiday in Étretat for the last two weeks.'

'At his stepmother's?'

'No. He doesn't see her. I think they fell out. He has a room at Les Roches Blanches, the hotel you can just see from here.'

'So he didn't go to La Bicoque?'

'Hold on. When Charles Besson—'

Poor Castaing sighed, despairing of being able to present a clear picture of the situation, especially since Maigret didn't appear to be listening.

'On Sunday morning Charles Besson arrived at around eleven with his wife and four children. They have a car, a big, early-model Panhard. Arlette had got there before them. They all had lunch at La Bicoque. Then Charles Besson went down to the beach with his eldest two, a fifteen-year-old boy and a twelve-year-old girl, while the ladies chatted.'

'Did he meet his brother?'

'He did. I suspect that Charles Besson suggested going for a walk so he could go and have a drink at the casino. From what people say he's fond of a tipple. He ran into Théo, whom he didn't know was in Étretat, and insisted on inviting him back to La Bicoque. Théo eventually gave in. So the entire family was there for dinner, a cold meal comprising lobster and leg of lamb.'

'No one was ill?'

'No. Other than the family, there was only the maid. Charles Besson and his family left at around half past nine. A five-year-old kid, Claude, had been sleeping in Valentine's bedroom, and, just before they got into the car, they had to give the baby a bottle. He's only six months old and he was crying.'

'What's the name of Charles Besson's wife?'

'I imagine it's Émilienne, she's called Mimi.'

'Mimi,' Maigret repeated gravely, as if learning a lesson by heart.

'She's a strapping brunette of around forty.'

'Strapping brunette, right! They drove off in their Panhard at around nine.'

'That's right. Théo stayed a few minutes longer, and then only the three women were left in the house.'

'Valentine, her daughter Arlette and young Rose.'

'Correct. Young Rose did the washing-up in the kitchen while the mother and daughter chatted in the living room.'

'Are all the bedrooms upstairs?'

'Except the guest room, as I told you, which is downstairs, with windows overlooking the garden. You'll see. It's like a doll's house, with tiny little rooms.'

'Arlette didn't go upstairs to her mother's room?'

'They went up together at around ten, because the old lady wanted to show her daughter a dress she'd just had made.'

'Did they both come back downstairs?'

'Yes. Then Valentine went up again to retire, followed, a few minutes later, by young Rose. She usually helped her mistress get into bed and gave her her medicine.'

'Was it she who prepared it?'

'No. Valentine put the drops in the glass of water beforehand.'

'Arlette didn't go back upstairs?'

'No. It was around eleven thirty when young Rose went to bed too.'

'And it was around two o'clock that she began to groan.'

'That's the time given by Arlette and her mother.'

'And, in your opinion, between midnight and two o'clock, there was a man in Arlette's bedroom, a man with whom she had driven from Paris. Do you happen to know how Théo spent his evening?'

'I haven't had the time to investigate yet. I confess I hadn't thought of it.'

'How about some lunch?'

'With pleasure.'

'Do you think I could have mussels?'

'Possibly, but I wouldn't count on it. I'm beginning to know the menu by heart.'

'This morning, did you go into Rose's parents' house?'

'Only into the front room, which had been turned into a chapel of rest.'

'Do you know if they have a good portrait of her?'

'I can ask them.'

'Do so. As many photographs as you can find, even as a child, at all ages. How old was she, by the way?'

'Twenty-two or twenty-three. I didn't write the report and—'

'I gather she'd been with the old lady for a very long time.'

'For seven years. She started working for her when she was very young, when Ferdinand Besson was still alive. She was a strong, buxom girl with a ruddy complexion.'

'She'd never been ill?'

'Doctor Jolly didn't mention anything. I think he'd have told me if she had.'

'I'd like to know whether she had any sweethearts, or a lover.'

'That did occur to me. Apparently not. She was very hardworking, she practically never went out.'

'Because she wasn't allowed out?'

'I think, but I could be wrong, that Valentine kept her on a tight rein and was reluctant to allow her any time off.'

All this time they'd been walking along the seafront. Maigret had been gazing constantly at the sea and hadn't thought about it for a moment.

It was already over. He had experienced a familiar little thrill that morning, in Bréauté-Beuzeville. The toy train had brought back memories of past holidays.

Now he no longer noticed the women's pastel bathing costumes, the children crouching among the pebbles; he was oblivious to the kelp's salty tang.

He had barely bothered to find out if there'd be mussels for lunch!

He was there, his head filled with new names which he tried to file away in his memory as he would have done in his office at Quai des Orfèvres. He and Castaing sat down at a table with a white cloth and gladioli in an imitation crystal fluted vase.

Maybe it was a sign that he was growing old? He craned to catch another glimpse of the white-crested waves, and it saddened him not to feel the slightest excitement.

'Were there a lot of people at the funeral?'

'The whole of Yport was there, as well as people who'd come from Étretat, Les Loges, Vaucottes, and the fishermen from Fécamp.'

Maigret recalled country funerals, had the impression he caught a whiff of Calvados and said very gravely:

'The men will all be drunk tonight.'

'That's fairly likely!' conceded Castaing, slightly taken aback by the famous inspector's train of thought.

There were no mussels on the menu, and so they had an hors-d'œuvre of canned sardines and celeriac remoulade.

2. *Valentine's Early Life*

He pushed open the unlocked gate and, seeing no bell, walked into the garden. He had never seen such a profusion of plants in a space so confined. The flowering shrubs were so close together that they created the impression of a jungle and in the tiniest space between them sprang dahlias, lupins, chrysanthemums and other flowers that Maigret recognized only from brightly coloured illustrations on seed packets in shop windows; and it looked as if the old lady had used every single packet.

The house whose slate roof he had glimpsed from the road was no longer visible above the greenery. The path zigzagged and, at one point, he must have turned right instead of left, because after a few steps he found himself in a courtyard with big pink flagstones on to which opened the kitchen and the laundry.

He saw a sturdy country woman dressed in black, with a few streaks of grey in her dark hair, her flesh and her eyes hard, beating a mattress. Around her, in the open air, stood a jumble of bedroom furniture, a bedside table with its drawer open, curtains and blankets hanging from a washing line, a straw-bottomed chair and a dismantled bed.

The woman looked at him without stopping her work.

'Is Madame Besson at home?'

She merely indicated the leaded windows surrounded by Virginia creeper; as he approached he could see Valentine in her sitting room. Unaware of his presence, since she wasn't expecting him to arrive via the courtyard, she was visibly preparing to receive him. Having placed a silver tray with a crystal decanter and glasses on a pedestal table, she stood back to gauge the effect, then looked at herself and tidied her hair in front of an antique mirror with a carved frame.

'Just knock,' said the country woman brusquely.

He hadn't noticed that one of the windows was in fact a casement door, and he knocked on it. Valentine turned round, surprised, and immediately produced a smile.

'I knew you'd come, but I had hoped to greet you at the main door, so to speak, although the term is a bit grand for this house.'

Right away, she made the same impression on him as she had in Paris. She was so animated, so sparkling that she had the air of a woman who was still young, very young even, disguised as an old lady for an amateur theatre production. And yet she wasn't trying to make herself look younger. On the contrary, the cut of her black silk dress, her hairstyle, the broad velvet choker that she wore round her neck were all typical of her age.

And, looking at her close up, he could see the delicate wrinkles, the withering of the neck, a certain dryness of her hands that left no doubt.

'Would you like to give me your hat, inspector, and see if there's an armchair that's the right size for you? You probably feel awkward in my doll's house, don't you?'

The charming thing about her was perhaps that she always seemed to be laughing at herself.

'You must have been told, or you will be, that I'm neurotic, and it's true that I've got all sorts of obsessions. You can't imagine how busy obsessions keep you when you live alone. Why don't you try that armchair over there, by the window? And do please smoke your pipe. My husband smoked cigars from dawn till dusk, and nothing permeates the house like cigar smoke. Between you and me, I don't think he really liked it. He only began smoking cigars very late, when he was well over forty, when Juva cream became famous.'

And hastily, as if to excuse her unkind comment:

'We all have our weaknesses. I imagine you had coffee at the hotel? Perhaps you'll allow me to offer you a Calvados that's over thirty years old?'

He had realized that it was her eyes as much as her vivacity that made her appear so young. They were of a blue that was paler than the September sky over the sea and still had an expression of surprise, of wonderment, the look of an Alice in Wonderland.

'I'll have a drop too, to keep you company, as long as you're not shocked. You see that I make no secret of my little vices. You'll find the house all topsy-turvy. I'm only just back from the funeral of poor young Rose. I found it very difficult to persuade Madame Leroy to come and give me a hand. You've probably guessed that it's the furniture from Rose's room you saw outside. I have a horror of death, inspector, and of everything associated with it. Until the house has been cleaned from top to bottom and aired for a few days I feel as though the stench of death will linger in the air.'

Shafts of sunlight shone through the branches of a linden tree and the small windowpanes, shedding flickering patches of light on to the objects in the room.

'I never imagined that one day the famous Inspector Maigret would sit in that armchair.'

'By the way, didn't you say that you'd kept newspaper articles about me?'

'That's right. I often used to cut them out, the way I used to cut out the serial stories from my father's newspaper.'

'Do you have them here?'

'I think I know where they are.'

He had sensed a hesitation in her voice. She went over with a forced naturalness to an antique writing desk and rummaged through the drawers in vain, then went to a carved chest.

'I think I put them in my bedroom.'

She moved to go upstairs.

'Don't put yourself to any trouble.'

'It's no trouble! I insist on finding them. I can guess what you're thinking. You imagine that I said that to you in Paris to flatter you and persuade you to come. It's true that I lie sometimes, like all women, but I promise you I'm speaking the truth.'

He heard her pottering around upstairs and, when she came back down again, she put on a rather exaggerated show of disappointment.

'Between you and me, Rose wasn't very tidy; she was

even what I call muddle-headed. Tomorrow I'll go and search the attic. In any case, I'll lay my hands on those articles before you leave Étretat. Now I expect you have lots of questions you want to ask me, so I'll go and sit quietly in my granny chair. To your good health, Monsieur Maigret.'

'To your good health, madame.'

'You don't think I'm too silly?'

He politely shook his head.

'You're not angry with me for having dragged you away from your Quai des Orfèvres? It's funny that my stepson had the same idea as me, isn't it? Being a politician, which he's so proud of, he went about things differently and spoke directly to the minister. Tell me honestly, is it because of him or me that you're here?'

'Because of you, most definitely.'

'Do you think I should be worried? It's funny! I simply can't take this threat seriously. People say that old women are fearful; I wonder why, when so many old women like me live alone in remote places. Rose slept here, but she was the one who was scared and came and woke me up at night when she thought she heard a noise. When there was a storm, she'd take refuge in my room and stay till morning sitting in my wing chair in her nightdress, mumbling prayers and quaking.

'If I've never been afraid, it's perhaps because I have no idea who could bear me a grudge. I'm not even wealthy any more. Everyone around here knows that I live on a modest annuity that survived the calamity. This house is also an annuity and no one will inherit it. I don't think I've ever done anyone harm . . .'

'All the same, Rose is dead.'

'That's true. This might make me sound stupid or selfish, but as time goes by, and now that she's buried, I find it hard to believe. In a while, no doubt, you'll go round the house. You see the dining room, next door. This other door opens into the guest room, where my daughter slept. Apart from the kitchen, the laundry and the tool shed, that's all there is downstairs, and upstairs is even smaller because there's nothing above the kitchen and the laundry.'

'Does your daughter often come to visit you?'

She gave a resigned little pout.

'Once a year, on my birthday. The rest of the time, I neither see her nor hear any news of her. She rarely writes either.'

'She's married to a dentist, I believe?'

'I expect you're going to need to know the entire family history, and that's only natural. Do you like honesty, Monsieur Maigret, or would you rather I answered you like a well-brought-up lady?'

'Do you need to ask?'

'You haven't met Arlette yet?'

'Not yet.'

She went over to a drawer and took out some envelopes containing photographs, each envelope reserved for a specific category of portraits.

'Look! This is her at eighteen. People say she resembles me and, as far as her features go, I have to acknowledge it's true.'

The likeness was striking. As slim as her mother, the girl

had the same delicate features and in particular the same big, pale blue eyes.

'She looks as if butter wouldn't melt in her mouth, doesn't she? Poor Julien was taken in by her and married her despite my warnings. He's a good boy, hardworking; he started out with nothing and struggled to finish his studies. He works ten hours a day and more in his cheap practice in Rue Saint-Antoine.'

'Do you think they are unhappy?'

'He may be happy after all. There are people who make their own happiness. Every Sunday he sets up his easel somewhere by the Seine and he paints. They have a canoe near Corbeil.'

'Does your daughter love her husband?'

'Look at the photos of her and answer the question yourself. Maybe she's capable of loving someone, but I have certainly never noticed it. When I used to work at the Seuret sisters' patisserie – you must have been told about that – she would sometimes say to me: "Do you think it's nice for me to have a mother who sells cakes to my friends!"

'She was seven when she said that. The two of us were living in a little room above a watchmaker's shop that's still there today.

'When I remarried, her life changed.'

'Would you mind telling me about your first husband?

'I expect others will talk to me about him, and I'd rather hear it from you.'

She refilled his glass, not at all taken aback by the question.

'I may as well begin with my parents, in that case. I was born Fouque, a name you'll still find in these parts. My father was a fisherman, here in Étretat. My mother worked as a domestic help in houses like this one, only during the summer, because in those days no one stayed during the winter. I had three brothers and one sister, who all died. One of my brothers was killed during the First World War and another died from his injuries in a boating accident. My sister got married and died in childbirth. As for my third brother, Lucien, who worked in Paris as a hairdresser's assistant, he went off the rails and was stabbed to death in a café near Bastille.

'I'm not ashamed of it. I have never denied my roots. If I'd been ashamed, I wouldn't have come to end my days here, where everyone knows my past.'

'Did you work while your parents were alive?'

'I was a nursery maid at fourteen, then a chambermaid at the Hôtel de la Plage. My mother died at that time, of breast cancer. My father lived to a fairly ripe old age, but he drank so much towards the end that it was as though he was no longer alive. I met a young man from Rouen who was a post-office clerk, Henri Poujolle, and I married him. He was kind, very gentle, well brought up, and I didn't realize at the time what the bright pink spots on his cheeks meant. For four years I played the little lady in a two-bedroom apartment, then the mother. I went to meet him from work pushing Baby's pram. On Sundays we bought a cake at the Seuret sisters' shop.

'Once a year we went to Rouen to visit my parents-in-law, who had a little grocery in the upper town.

'Then Henri began coughing, and he died within a few months, leaving me alone with Arlette.

'I moved home, making do with just one room. I went to see the Seuret sisters and they took me on as an assistant.

'People say I was fresh and pretty, and that I brought in the customers.

'One day, in the shop, I made the acquaintance of Ferdinand Besson.'

'How old were you?'

'When we were married, a few months later, I was thirty.'

'What about him?'

'Around fifty-five. He'd been a widower for several years, and had two boys of sixteen and eighteen, and that's what was the strangest thing for me, because I always had the feeling that they were about to fall in love.'

'And they didn't?'

'Théo, maybe, at first. Then he took a sudden dislike to me, but I never bore him a grudge. You know Besson's story?'

'I know he was the owner of Juva beauty products.'

'So you probably think he was someone extraordinary? But the truth is very different. He was a small-time pharmacist in Le Havre, a very ordinary local pharmacist with a narrow, dingy shop that had a green jar and a yellow jar in the window. He himself, at forty, as you'll see from his photo, looked more like a gas engineer, and his wife looked like a cleaning woman.

'In those days there weren't as many specialist products

as there are today and he had to make up all sorts of preparations for his customers. That was how he came to mix a cream for a girl who had always had a spotty face. The cream worked wonders for her. The whole neighbourhood heard about it, and then the whole town.

'One of Besson's brothers-in-law advised him to market the product under a fancy name and between them they came up with "Juva". It was the brother-in-law who provided the initial funding.

'Almost overnight he made a fortune. He had to build laboratories, first of all in Le Havre, then in Pantin, outside Paris. The name "Juva" was in all the papers, then it appeared on the walls in giant letters.

'You can't imagine how much those products make, once they're on the market.

'Besson's first wife barely benefited, because she died shortly afterwards.

'He began to change his lifestyle. By the time I met him he was already a very wealthy man, but he wasn't used to having money and he wasn't sure what to do with it.

'I think that's why he married me.'

'What do you mean?'

'That he needed a pretty wife to dress and show off. Parisian women frightened him and he was intimidated by the bourgeois ladies of Le Havre. He felt more at ease with a girl he'd met serving in a patisserie. I don't think he even minded my being a widow, or that I too had a child.

'I don't know if you understand what I'm saying?'

He did, but what surprised him was that she had grasped it so well and that she had accepted so amiably.

'Immediately after our wedding he bought a townhouse in Avenue d'Iéna and, a few years later, the Château d'Anzi, in Sologne. He showered me with jewellery, sent me to dressmakers, took me to the theatre and to the races. He even had a yacht built, which he never sailed because he suffered from seasickness.'

'Do you think he was happy?'

'I don't know. In his office, Rue Tronchet, he probably was, because he was surrounded by subordinates. I think in fact that he always felt that people were laughing at him. And yet he was a good man, as clever as most big businessmen. Perhaps he had begun to have a lot of money too late.

'He got it into his head to become a captain of industry and, alongside Juva cream, which was a goldmine, he decided to create other products: a toothpaste, a soap, I don't know what else, and spent millions on advertising them. He built factories to make not only the products themselves but also the packaging. And Théo, who came into the business, was perhaps even more ambitious than he was.

'It lasted twenty-five years, Monsieur Maigret. Now I can barely remember it, the time passed so quickly. We were always in a hurry. We went from our house in Paris to our chateau, and from there to Cannes or Nice, and then we hared back to Paris, with two motor cars, one for the luggage, the butler, the maids and the cook.

'Then he decided to go travelling every year, and we went to London and Scotland, Turkey, Egypt, always in a rush because he needed to get back and attend to his business, always with trunks full of dresses and my jewellery, which we had to put in a bank safe deposit box in every city we visited.

'Arlette got married. I've never known why. Or rather I've never known why she suddenly married that boy whom we hadn't even met, when she could have taken her pick from among the rich young men who were frequent visitors to our house.'

'Did your husband have a soft spot for your daughter?'

'You're wondering whether it wasn't a bit more than a soft spot, aren't you? I wondered about that too. It seems natural that a man of a certain age, living with a young girl who is not his daughter, should fall in love with her. I kept an eye on the pair of them. It's true that he spoiled her with gifts and gave in to her every wish. I never came across anything else. No! And I have no idea why Arlette got married, at twenty, to the first comer. I understand many people, but I've never understood my own daughter.'

'Do you get on well with your stepsons?'

'Théo, the eldest, soon gave me the cold shoulder, but Charles always treated me as if I were his mother. Théo never married. In other words, for a number of years he enjoyed the life that his father wasn't able to live, not having been to the manner born. Why are you looking at me like that?'

Because of the contrast again. She spoke lightly, with a faint smile, with the same candid expression in her light-coloured eyes, and he was amazed at the words that came out of her mouth.

'I've had the time to think, you know, during the five years I've lived alone here! So Théo used to go to the races, was a regular at Maxim's, Fouquet's, all the fashionable places, and spent his summers in Deauville. In those days he kept an open table, always surrounded by young people who had famous names but no money. He still has the same lifestyle, or rather frequents the same places, but now he's the one who's broke and has to rely on others to pay for him. I don't know how he manages it.'

'You weren't surprised to learn he was in Étretat?'

'We hadn't spoken to each other for years. I spotted him in town, two weeks ago, and I thought he was just passing through. Then, on Sunday, Charles brought him here and asked the two of us to make peace, and I held out my hand to him.'

'He didn't give you any reason for his presence here?'

'He simply said that he needed a rest. But you interrupted me. I was telling you about the time when my husband was still alive, and his last ten years were no fun.'

'When did he buy you this house?'

'Before everything began to go downhill, when we already had the mansion in Paris, the chateau and the whole caboodle. It was me who asked him for a pied-à-terre here, where I feel more at home than anywhere else.'

Did a smile escape him? She hastily added:

'I know what you're thinking, and perhaps you are not entirely mistaken. At Anzi I played the lady, as Ferdinand asked me to do. I presided over all the good works, all the ceremonies, but no one knew who I was. It felt unfair that no one could see me in my new life in the town where I had been poor and humble. That might not be very nice, but I think it's only human.

'You may as well hear it from me, because everyone else is bound to tell you, that some people call me the Chatelaine – not without a hint of irony.

'Behind my back they prefer to call me simply Valentine!

'I never understood anything about business, but it's clear that Ferdinand was over-ambitious and did not always make the right decisions, perhaps not so much to impress others as to prove to himself that he was a big-time financier.

'First we sold the yacht, then the chateau. One night after the dance I gave him my pearls to put in the safe and he said with a bitter smile:

'"It's better, for the sake of appearances, but it wouldn't be a tragedy if they were stolen because they're only imitations."

'He became taciturn, withdrawn. Only Juva cream still thrived, while his new businesses went under one after the other.'

'Did he love his sons?'

'I don't know. That might sound strange to you. People imagine that parents love their children. It seems natural. But I actually wonder whether the opposite isn't true more often than we think.

'He was certainly pleased to see Théo accepted in social circles where he couldn't dream of being welcome himself. He must have realized, on the other hand, that Théo was worthless and that his grand ideas were largely to blame for the disaster.

'As for Charles, he never forgave him for being spineless, because he had an absolute horror of spineless, weak people.'

'Because deep down he was weak too, is that what you're saying?'

'Yes. The fact remains that his last years were sad, seeing everything he had built up fall apart, piece by piece. Perhaps he truly loved me? He wasn't very communicative and I don't recall ever hearing him call me "darling". He was keen to ensure I wouldn't want for anything financially: he took out a life annuity on this house and arranged a small allowance before he died. That is pretty much all he left. His children only received a few mementos of no value, as did my daughter. He treated her just like his sons.'

'Did he die here?'

'No. He died alone in a hotel room in Paris, where he had gone in the hope of negotiating a new business deal. He was seventy. So now you're becoming acquainted with the family. I don't know what Théo does exactly, but he always has a little motor car; he's well dressed and lives in elegant places. As for Charles, who has four children and a wife who's not particularly pleasant, he has tried several professions without success. His pet project was to found a newspaper, but this failed in both Rouen and Le Havre. Next he got involved in a business in Fécamp, making fertilizer from fish waste; then, since that was going reasonably well, he put himself forward on some list for the elections.

'He was voted in by sheer luck, and lo and behold he's been a politician for two years.

'None of them is a saint, but they're not bad people either.

'Although they might not love me unconditionally, I

don't think they hate me, and none of them would stand to gain from my death.

'The knick-knacks you see wouldn't fetch much at auction and they are all I own, together with the replicas of my jewellery.

'As for the local people, they think I'm an old dear and see me as part of the landscape.

'Nearly everyone I knew as a girl has died. There are only a few surviving old folk, like the elder Seuret sister, whom I visit from time to time.

'That someone should get it into their head to poison me seems so unlikely, so absurd that I'm a little embarrassed to have brought you here and I'm ashamed now of having gone to see you in Paris.

'You must have taken me for a batty old woman, admit it!'

'No.'

'Why not? What made you take it seriously?'

'Young Rose is dead!'

'That's true.'

She glanced out of the window at the furniture scattered around the courtyard and the blankets hanging from the washing line.

'Is your gardener here today?'

'No. Yesterday was his day.'

'Did the cleaner carry the furniture down on her own?'

'We took it apart and brought it down together early this morning, before I went to Yport.'

The furniture was heavy and the staircase narrow, with an awkward bend.

'I am stronger than I appear, Monsieur Maigret. I look as if I have the bones of a bird, and it's true, my bones are small. But even though she was sturdy, Rose was no stronger than I am.'

She got up to refill his glass again and poured herself a drop of the aged amber Calvados, whose aroma filled the room.

She was taken aback by the question Maigret asked as he calmly puffed on his pipe:

'Do you think that your son-in-law – Julien Sudre, he's called, isn't he? – turns a blind eye to his wife's goings on?'

Astonished, she laughed.

'I've never asked myself.'

'And you've never asked yourself either whether your daughter had one or several lovers?'

'My goodness, that wouldn't surprise me.'

'On Sunday night there was a man here in the guest room with your daughter.'

She frowned and thought.

'Now I understand.'

'What do you understand?'

'Certain details that didn't strike me at the time. All day Arlette was distracted, preoccupied. After lunch she offered to take Charles' children for a walk along the beach and looked disappointed when he wanted to go himself. When I asked her why her husband hadn't come with her, she told me that he had a landscape to finish by the Seine.

'"Are you staying the night?" I asked.

'"I don't know. I don't think so. It's probably best if I take the evening train back."

'I urged her to stay. Several times I caught her looking out of the window, and I remember now that at nightfall a motor car drove past the house two or three times almost at a crawl.'

'What did you women talk about?'

'It's hard to say. Mimi had to take care of her baby, which needed changing several times. She also had to prepare the bottle, calm Claude, who's five and who was damaging the flower beds. We talked about the children, naturally. Arlette remarked to Mimi that the youngest must have come as a surprise, after five years, when the eldest was already fifteen, and Mimi replied that Charles never surprised her in any other way, and then she was the one who was lumbered . . .

'You can imagine! We swapped recipes.'

'Did Arlette go up to your room after dinner?'

'Yes, I wanted to show her a dress I'd had made recently, and I tried it on in front of her.'

'Where was she standing?'

'She was sitting on the bed.'

'Was she alone at any point?'

'Perhaps for a few seconds while I was fetching the dress from the little room that serves as my linen room. But I can't imagine that Arlette would pour poison in my sleeping potion. She'd have had to open the medicine cabinet which is in the bathroom. I would have heard her. And why would Arlette have done that? So, she's unfaithful to poor old Julien?'

'A man visited Arlette in her bedroom after midnight and must have left hurriedly via the window when he heard Rose's groans.'

She couldn't help laughing.

'That was bad timing!'

But thinking about it retrospectively did not frighten her.

'Who is it, someone from around here?'

'Someone who drove her here from Paris in a car, a certain Hervé Peyrot, who's in the wine trade.'

'Young?'

'Fortyish.'

'I must say I was surprised she came by train when her husband has a car and she drives. All this is very bizarre, Monsieur Maigret. As a matter of fact, I'm glad you're here. The inspector took away the glass and the medicine bottle, as well as various items from my room and the bathroom. I'm curious to know what the laboratory people will discover. Some plainclothes police officers came too and took photos. If only young Rose hadn't been so stubborn! I told her the medicine had a strange taste and once she'd left the room, she still drank the remains. She didn't need anything to help her sleep, I assure you. How many times did I lie there listening to her snoring through the partition as soon as her head touched the pillow! Perhaps you'd like to have a look around the house?'

He had been there for barely an hour and he already felt as if he knew it, as if it was familiar. The starchy figure of the cleaning woman – a widow for certain – appeared in the doorway.

'Will you eat the rest of the stew this evening or shall I give it to the cat?'

She said this almost spitefully, without smiling.

'I'll eat it, Madame Leroy.'

'I've finished outside. Everything's clean. When you're ready to help me carry the furniture back upstairs . . .'

Valentine gave Maigret a half-smile.

'Later.'

'But I don't have anything else to do.'

'Then rest for a minute.'

And she preceded him up the narrow staircase that smelled of wax polish.

3. *Arlette's Lovers*

'Drop in and see me whenever you like, Monsieur Maigret. After bringing you here from Paris, the very least I can do is remain at your disposal. I hope you aren't too annoyed with me for having put you to so much trouble over this ridiculous business?'

They were in the garden, just as Maigret was leaving. The widow Leroy was still waiting for her mistress to help her carry the furniture back into Rose's room. Maigret was on the verge of offering to help, because he couldn't imagine Valentine humping such a heavy load.

'I'm surprised now that I urged you to come, because I'm not even afraid.'

'Is Madame Leroy going to sleep here?'

'Oh no! She'll be going home in an hour's time. She has a twenty-four-year-old son who works for the railways. She pampers him like a baby. It's because he'll be home soon that she can't keep still.'

'Will you sleep in the house alone?'

'It won't be the first time.'

He had crossed the little garden and pushed open the gate, which squeaked. The sun was setting over the sea, bathing the path in yellow light, already reddening. The unsurfaced road was bordered by hedgerows and nettles, like those of his childhood, and his feet stumbled in the soft dust.

A little further down was the beginning of a bend and rounding this bend he saw, coming towards him, the shape of a woman toiling up the slope.

Her back was to the light and she wore dark clothes, and he immediately knew who she was. There was no doubt it was Arlette, the old lady's daughter. She did not look as tiny and slim as her mother, but she had the same delicateness, seemed to be made of the same fragile, precious stuff, and she had the same huge eyes of an incredible blue.

Did she recognize Maigret, whose photograph had so often been in the newspapers? Or did she simply say to herself, on seeing a stranger dressed like a city dweller on this road, that he could only be a police officer?

Maigret had the impression that during the brief moment when they passed each other she hesitated as if about to speak to him. He too hesitated. He wanted to speak to her, but this was neither the right time nor the right place.

So they merely looked at one another in silence, and Arlette's eyes expressed no emotion. They were solemn and there was something faraway, something impersonal in her gaze. Maigret turned around when she had already disappeared behind the hedge, then continued on his way until he reached the first streets of Étretat.

He ran into Inspector Castaing in front of a display of postcards.

'I was waiting for you, sir. I've just received the reports. They're here, in my pocket. Do you want to read them?'

'What I'd like more than anything is to sit down at a terrace and drink a glass of cold beer.'

'Didn't she offer you a drink?'

'She gave me a Calvados that was so old, so excellent that it's made me thirsty for something more ordinary and thirst-quenching.'

The sun, which from mid-afternoon had been slipping down like a huge red ball, heralded the end of summer, as did the dwindling number of holidaymakers, who were already wearing woollen clothes and, now driven from the beach by the coolness, didn't know what to do with themselves in town.

'Arlette has just arrived,' said Maigret when they were installed at a pedestal table on Place de la Mairie.

'Did you see her?'

'I presume that this time she came by train.'

'Did she go to her mother's? Did you talk to her?'

'We simply passed each other around a hundred metres from La Bicoque.'

'Do you think she's going to sleep there?'

'I think it's likely.'

'There's no one else in the house, is there?'

'Tonight there will only be the mother and the daughter.'

This worried the inspector.

'You're not going to make me read all these papers, are you?' said Maigret, pushing away the bulging yellow envelope full of documents. 'Tell me about the glass, first of all. You're the one who found it and packaged it up?'

'Yes. It was in the maid's room, on the bedside table. I asked Madame Besson if it was the one that had contained her medicine. Apparently there's no mistaking it, because the glass is slightly tinted; it's the last remaining one from an old set.'

'Fingerprints?'

'The old lady's and Rose's.'

'The bottle?'

'I found the sleeping potion in the medicine chest in the bathroom, where I'd been told it was kept. It had only the old lady's prints on it. Did you see her bedroom, by the way?'

Like Maigret, Castaing had been surprised on entering Valentine's room. She had let the detective chief inspector in with a cheerful ease, without a word, but she must have been aware of the effect the room would produce.

Since the rest of the house was pretty and in good taste, displaying a certain sophistication, visitors did not expect to find themselves in an extremely coquettish boudoir whose walls were covered with cream satin. In the midst of a huge bed a Persian cat with bluish fur was having a nap and barely opened his golden eyes to acknowledge the intruder.

'It's perhaps a rather ridiculous room for an old woman, isn't it?'

When they had moved into the yellow-tiled bathroom, she added:

'It's probably because when I was young I never had my own bedroom. I had to share an attic room with my sisters and we had to go and wash in the courtyard, on the edge of the well. In Avenue d'Iéna, Ferdinand had a pink marble bathroom put in for me. All the fittings were silver gilt and there was a sunken bath with three steps down.'

Rose's room, with its waxed floor and floral wallpapers, was empty and there was a draught blowing that made the cretonne curtains billow like crinolines.

'What did the coroner say?'

'There's no doubt she was poisoned. A high dose of arsenic. The sleeping draught did not cause the maid's death. The report adds that the liquid must have had a very bitter taste.'

'That's what Valentine said too.'

'But Rose drank it all the same. Do you see that man over the road, walking towards the stationer's? That's Théo Besson.'

He was a tall, big-boned man with strongly defined features and looked around fifty. He wore a very English-looking rust-coloured tweed jacket. He was bareheaded, his hair grey and sparse.

He spotted the two men. He knew the inspector already and most likely recognized Detective Chief Inspector Maigret. He hesitated, as Arlette had done, gave a slight nod in greeting and went inside the stationer's.

'Have you interviewed him?'

'In passing. I asked him if there was anything he wanted to tell me and whether he intended to stay in Étretat for long. He replied that he had no plans to leave town before the hotel closes on the 15th of September.'

'How does he spend his days?'

'He often walks along the coast, alone, with big, regular strides, like people of a certain age who want to stay fit.

'He goes for a swim at around eleven and hangs around the casino bar or in the cafés the rest of the time.'

'Does he drink a lot?'

'Ten or so whiskies a day, but I don't think he gets drunk. He reads four or five newspapers. Sometimes he gambles, without ever sitting down at one of the gaming tables.'

'Nothing else in these reports?'

'Nothing of interest.'

'Has Théo Besson seen his stepmother since Sunday?'

'Not as far as I know.'

'Who has seen her? Give me a summary of what happened on Monday. I've more or less got an idea of the Sunday, but I can't quite picture the events of Monday.'

He knew how Valentine had spent Tuesday because she had told him. She'd left La Bicoque early and caught the first train to Paris, leaving Madame Leroy on her own. On arrival, he'd taken a taxi to Quai des Orfèvres, where she'd called on Maigret.

'Did you go and see your daughter afterwards?' he'd asked her earlier.

'No. Why?'

'Do you ever visit her when you're in Paris?'

'Seldom. They have their life and I have mine. Besides, I don't like the Saint-Antoine neighbourhood, where they live, or their pretentious apartment.'

'What did you do?'

'I had luncheon in a restaurant in Rue Duphot, where I've always liked to eat, did some shopping in the Madeleine area, then caught my train home.'

'Did your daughter know you were in Paris?'

'No.'

'Nor your stepson Charles?'

'I didn't tell them about my idea.'

Now he really wanted to know what had happened on the Monday.

'When I arrived, at around eight o'clock,' said Castaing, 'I found the household in quite a state, as you can imagine.'

'Who was there?'

'Madame Besson, of course.'

'Wearing what?'

'Her usual outfit. Her daughter was there too, in her slippers, her hair unbrushed. Doctor Jolly was sitting with them, a man of a certain age, a family friend, calm, level-headed, and the elderly gardener had just arrived. As for Charles Besson, he was just a few steps ahead of me.'

'Who told you what had happened?'

'Valentine. From time to time the doctor interrupted her to ask about an important detail. She told me that she was the one who'd asked someone to telephone her stepson to let him know. He was very upset, "devastated". He seemed relieved that the press hadn't shown up yet and that the locals weren't aware of anything. You've just seen his brother. He's very much like him, only fatter and flabbier.

'The fact that there's no telephone in the house made my job more difficult, because I had to call Le Havre several times and each time I had to come into town.

'The doctor left first because he had patients to see.'

'Weren't Rose's parents informed?'

'No. It didn't occur to anybody to tell them. It was me who went to Yport to see them. One of her brothers came back with me, and her mother.'

'How did that go?'

'Not well. The mother glared at Madame Besson as if she blamed her for what had happened and refused to speak to her. As for the brother, I don't know what Charles Besson said to him, but he flew off the handle.

'"We must know the truth. Don't you think I'll allow this to be hushed up because you can pull a few strings!"

'They wanted to take the body to Yport. I had a great deal of difficulty convincing them that first of all it had to be transferred to Le Havre for the autopsy.

'At that point the father arrived on his bicycle. He didn't say a word to anyone. He's a short, stocky man, very strong, very solidly built. As soon as the body was loaded into the van, he took his family away. Charles Besson offered to drive them home in his car, but they refused, and the three of them left on foot, the old man pushing his bicycle.

'I can't vouch for the exact timing of what I'm telling you. Neighbours began to arrive, then people from the town were swarming all over the garden. I was upstairs with Cornu, from Criminal Records, who was taking photos and looking for fingerprints.

'When I came back downstairs, at around midday, I couldn't see Arlette and her mother told me she'd gone back to Paris for fear her husband would be worried.

'Charles Besson stayed until three o'clock and then returned to Fécamp.'

'Did he mention me?'

'No. Why?'

'He didn't tell you that he was planning to ask the minister to put me in charge of the investigation?'

'He didn't say anything to me, other than that he would handle the press. I can't think of anything else on the Monday. Oh yes! That evening, I spotted Théo Besson in the street. Someone pointed him out to me and I stopped to have a few words with him.

'"Have you heard what's happened at La Bicoque?" I asked him.

'"I've been told."

'"Do you have any information that might help our investigation?"

'"None whatsoever."

'He was very cold, distant. That was when I asked if he planned to leave Étretat and he replied as I've told you. Now, if you don't need me this evening, I'm going back to Le Havre to write my report. I promised my wife I'd have dinner with her if I could, because we have friends over.'

He had left his car outside the hotel and Maigret walked back with him through quiet streets. From time to time, as they rounded a bend, they had a view of the sea.

'Aren't you a little concerned that Arlette will be staying at her mother's tonight and the two women will be alone in the house?'

He was visibly preoccupied and, perhaps because Maigret was so calm, he felt that the latter was taking things lightly.

As the sun grew redder and the roofs of the houses appeared to be on fire, the sea took on an icy green colour and the world to the east of the setting sun seemed frozen in a surreal eternity.

'What time would you like me to be here tomorrow morning?'

'Not before nine. Perhaps you could telephone the Police Judiciaire for me to find out everything you can about Arlette Sudre and her husband. I'd also like to know what kind of life Charles Besson leads when he's in Paris and, while you're about it, ask if they have anything on Théo. Try and speak to Lucas. I don't like telephoning about these things from here.'

Most of the passers-by turned round to look at them and people watched them through the shop windows. Maigret didn't know how he was going to spend the evening yet, or how he would go about the investigation. From time to time he repeated mechanically to himself:

'Young Rose is dead.'

She was the only person about whom he knew nothing yet, other than that she had been plump and buxom.

'By the way,' he asked Castaing, who was pressing the starter, 'she must have had some personal belongings in her room at Valentine's. What's happened to them?'

'Her parents stuffed them into her suitcase and took it away.'

'Did you ask to see them?'

'I didn't dare. If you go and see them, you'll understand why. They weren't exactly friendly. They stare at you suspiciously and they look at one another before grunting a reply.'

'I'll probably go over there tomorrow.'

'I wouldn't be surprised if Charles Besson paid you a visit, since he took it upon himself to pester the minister to have you put in charge of the case!'

Castaing set off in his little car on the road to Le Havre, while Maigret, before going into his hotel, headed for the casino, whose terrace overlooked the beach. It was automatic. He was obeying that sort of impulse that prompts city dwellers, when they are by the sea, to sit and watch the sunset.

And all Étretat's remaining bathers were there, girls in pastel dresses, a few elderly ladies, looking out for the famous green ray that would shoot up as the red globe sank beneath the horizon.

Maigret gazed at the sky until his eyes ached but he didn't see the green ray. He went into the bar, where a familiar voice hailed him:

'What will it be, inspector?'

'Well, well! Charlie!'

A barman he had met in an establishment in Rue Daunou in Paris and whom he was surprised to find here.

'I was sure they'd send you to handle this case. What do you reckon?'

'What about you?'

'I think the old lady had a very narrow escape and the skivvy was unlucky.'

Maigret drank a Calvados, because he was in Normandy and he had started out on it. Charlie served other customers. Théo Besson came and sat on one of the high stools and unfolded a Paris newspaper which he had probably gone to buy at the station.

Apart from a few little clouds that were still pink, the world outside had lost all its colour, the infinite vastness of the sky forming a lid over the infinite sea.

'Young Rose is dead.'

Dead from having drunk medicine that wasn't prescribed for her and which she did not need.

He lingered a little longer, feeling sluggish from the Calvados, then he made his way back to his hotel, whose façade was a chalky white in the twilight. He walked past the pot plants on the steps and followed the red carpet to the reception counter where he intended to collect his key. The manager leaned towards him and said confidentially:

'There's a lady who's been waiting for you for some time.'

And he looked over towards the red-velvet armchairs in a corner of the lobby.

'I told her I didn't know when you'd be back, and she said she'd wait. She's . . .'

He muttered a name so quietly that Maigret couldn't hear. But, turning round, he recognized Arlette Sudre who, just then, rose from her chair.

He was more conscious of her elegance than he had been when they'd passed each other that afternoon, perhaps because she was the only person in town clothes, and she was wearing a very Parisian hat as if she were on her way to an afternoon tryst in the wealthy Madeleine district.

He walked towards her, feeling a little awkward.

'I'm the person you're waiting for, I believe? Detective Chief Inspector Maigret.'

'As you know, I am Arlette Sudre.'

He nodded to indicate that he did know. Then they were both silent for a moment. She looked about her to make him understand that it was difficult to talk there in the lobby, where an elderly couple were staring at them and straining to listen to their conversation.

'I presume you would like to speak to me in private. Unfortunately this isn't Quai des Orfèvres and I don't see where . . .'

He cast around. He couldn't invite her up to his room. The waitresses were laying the tables in the dining room, which seated 200 people, but where there were only around twenty diners.

'Perhaps the easiest thing would be if you had a bite to eat with me? I could choose a secluded table.'

She was more at ease than he was. She accepted his suggestion naturally, without thanking him, and followed him into the almost deserted dining room.

'May we have dinner?' he asked the waitress.

'In a few minutes. You can sit down if you like. Dinner for two?'

'Just a minute. May we have something to drink?'

He turned questioningly to Arlette.

'Martini,' she said half-heartedly.

'Two martinis.'

He still felt embarrassed, and it was not solely because the previous Sunday a man had spent part of the night in Arlette's room. She was the classic example of the pretty woman with whom a lucky man has an intimate dinner, eyeing the people coming in for fear of seeing someone he knows. And Maigret was going to have dinner with her here.

She sat gazing coolly at him, unforthcoming, as if it was up to him to speak and not her.

'So, you're back from Paris!' he said, growing tired of waiting.

'You must have guessed why?'

She was probably prettier than her mother had ever been, but, unlike Valentine, she did nothing to make herself agreeable. She remained aloof, and there was no warmth in her eyes.

'If you don't know yet, I'll tell you.'

'Do you mean Hervé?'

Their martinis arrived and she dipped her lips in hers, took a handkerchief out of her black suede handbag and automatically grabbed a lipstick, but didn't use it.

'What are you planning to do?' she asked, looking him straight in the eyes.

'I don't understand your question.'

'I don't have a lot of experience in these matters, but I do read the newspapers. When an accident like the one last Sunday night happens, the police usually poke around in the private lives of everyone involved, and it's barely better being innocent than guilty. Since I am married and I'm very fond of my husband, I am asking you what you intend to do.'

'About the handkerchief?'

'If you like.'

'Your husband doesn't know?'

He saw her lip tremble, with impatience or anger, and she said:

'You sound like my mother.'

'Because your mother thought that perhaps your husband knew about your extra-marital life?'

She gave a scornful little snigger.

'You choose your words carefully, don't you?'

'I'll be blunt, if you prefer. From what you've just said your mother thought your husband turned a blind eye.'

'She didn't think it, she said so.'

'As I don't know him from Adam or from Eve, I haven't had the opportunity to form an opinion. Now . . .'

She was still staring at him, and he felt an urge to provoke her:

'Well, you can only blame yourself if someone gets that idea. You're thirty-eight, aren't you? You've been married since the age of twenty. I find it hard to believe that your fling last Sunday was the first of its kind.'

She shot back:

'True, it's not the first.'

'You only had one night to spend at your mother's, and still you felt the need to bring your lover into the house.'

'Perhaps we don't often get the chance to spend the night together?'

'I'm not judging, I'm observing. Which is why I thought your husband knew.'

'He didn't and he still doesn't. That's the reason I came back after leaving in a hurry.'

'Why did you leave at midday on Monday?'

'I didn't know what'd happened to Hervé after he left the house when Rose started groaning. I didn't know what my husband would do when he heard the news. I wanted to avoid him coming here.'

'I understand. And once back in Paris, were you worried?'

'Yes. I telephoned Charles, who told me you were in charge of the investigation.'

'Did you find that reassuring?'

'No.'

'May I serve, sir? Madame?'

He nodded and they stopped talking until the soup was on the table.

'Will my husband find out?'

'It's unlikely. Not unless he has to.'

'Do you suspect me of attempting to poison my mother?'

Her spoon was poised in mid-air, and he looked at her with a mixture of astonishment and a hint of admiration.

'Why do you ask me that?'

'Because I was the only person in the house who could have put poison in the glass. Or, to be exact, I was the only person still in the house when it happened.'

'You mean that Mimi could have done it before she left?'

'Mimi or Charles, or even Théo. Only, inevitably, everyone thinks of me.'

'Why inevitably?'

'Because everyone is convinced that I don't love my mother.'

'And is it true?'

'More or less.'

'Would you mind very much if I asked you a few questions? Mind you, this is off the record. You're the one who came to see me.'

'You would have questioned me sooner or later, wouldn't you?'

'It's possible, and even probable.'

The elderly couple were sitting three tables away, and at another table was a middle-aged woman gazing dotingly at her eighteen-year-old son, fussing over him as if he were a child. Bursts of loud laughter came from a table of girls, in waves so it seemed.

Maigret and his companion spoke in hushed tones as they ate, outwardly calm, indifferent.

'Have you not loved your mother for a long time?'

'Since the day I realized that she'd never loved me, that I'd been an accident and she felt that I'd ruined her life.'

'When did you discover that?'

'When I was still a little girl. But I shouldn't only talk about myself. It's fair to say that Mother has never loved anyone, not even me.'

'Didn't she love your father either?'

'From the day he died there was no longer any mention of him. I defy you to find a single photograph of my father in the house. You were there earlier. You saw Mother's bedroom. Did anything strike you about it?'

He racked his memory and admitted:

'No.'

'It may be because you haven't visited many houses belonging to old women. In most of them you'll find hundreds of photographs on the walls and on the furniture.'

She was right. And yet he remembered one portrait, a portrait of an elderly man, in a beautiful silver frame on her bedside table.

'My stepfather,' she replied to his protest. 'First of all, she put it there mainly because of the frame. And then it's true that he was the former owner of Juva products, which counts for something. And lastly, he spent half his life pandering to my mother's every whim and giving her everything she possessed. Did you see any pictures of me? Or of my stepbrothers? Charles, for example, is obsessed with taking photographs of his children at every age and sending prints to the family. In my mother's house all those photos are in a drawer, with pencil stubs, old letters, cotton reels and goodness knows what. But on the walls are photos of her, of her motor cars, her chateau, her yacht, her cats, especially her cats.'

'I can see that you really don't like her!'

'I don't think I even hold it against her any more.'

'What?'

'It doesn't matter. However, if someone tried to poison her—'

'I'm sorry. You just said *if*.'

'Let's say it's a manner of speaking. Mind you, with Mother, you never know.'

'Are you insinuating that she could've pretended to have been poisoned?'

'It's true it wouldn't make sense, especially as there was poison in the glass, and enough to kill, because poor Rose is dead.'

'Did your stepbrothers and your sister-in-law share your . . . let's say your indifference, if not your antipathy, to your mother?'

'They don't have the same reasons as me. Mimi doesn't like her very much because she thinks that, had it not been for her, my stepfather wouldn't have lost his fortune.'

'Is that true?'

'I don't know. It's certain that it was on her that he spent the most money and that she was the one he particularly wanted to impress.'

'How did you get on with your stepfather?'

'Almost immediately after her marriage Mother sent me off to a very exclusive, very expensive boarding school in Switzerland, on the pretext that my father had suffered from tuberculosis and that it was important to look after my lungs.'

'Pretext?'

'I'd never coughed in my life. It was just that the presence of an adolescent girl annoyed her. Perhaps she was jealous too.'

'Of what?'

'Ferdinand tended to spoil me, pamper me. When I came back from Paris, at the age of seventeen, he began to hang around me insistently.'

'You mean . . .?'

'No. Not straight away. I was eighteen and a half when it happened, one evening when I was getting ready to go to the theatre; he came into my room when I wasn't completely dressed.'

'What happened?'

'Nothing. He lost his head and I slapped him. Then he fell at my feet and began to cry, begging me not to say anything to Mother, not to leave. He swore he'd had a moment of madness and that he'd never do it again.'

She added coldly:

'He was ridiculous, in tails, with his shirt front that'd

popped out of his waistcoat. He had to get up quickly because the maid was coming in.'

'Did you stay?'

'Yes.'

'Were you in love with someone?'

'Yes.'

'Whom?'

'Théo.'

'And was he in love with you?'

'He didn't take any notice of me. He had his bachelor pad on the ground floor, and I knew that although his father had forbidden it, he brought women home. I spent nights spying on him. There was one, a little dancer from the Théâtre du Châtelet, who, at one time, came almost every night. I hid in his apartment.'

'And did you make a scene?'

'I don't know what I did exactly, but she left, furious, and I was left alone with Théo.'

'Then what?'

'He didn't want to. I almost forced him.'

She spoke in a low voice, in such a natural tone that it sounded somewhat unreal, especially in these surroundings for respectable holidaymakers, with the waitress in her black dress and white apron interrupting them from time to time.

'And afterwards?' he repeated.

'There was no afterwards. We avoided one another.'

'Why?'

'He probably felt embarrassed.'

'What about you?'

'Because I was sick of men.'

'Is that why you married so hastily?'

'I didn't straight away. For more than a year I slept with all the men who came after me.'

'Out of revulsion?'

'Yes. You can't understand.'

'And then?'

'I realized that things would end badly; I was disgusted, I wanted to put an end to it.'

'By getting married?'

'By trying to live like everyone else.'

'And once married, you carried on?'

She looked at him solemnly and said:

'Yes.'

There was a long silence, during which the girls at the other table could be heard laughing.

'From the first year?'

'From the first month.'

'Why?'

'I don't know. Because I can't help it. Julien has never suspected, and I'd do anything to make sure he never finds out.'

'Do you love him?'

'Too bad if it makes you laugh. *Yes!* In any case, he is the only man I respect. Do you have any other questions you want to ask?'

'When I've taken in everything you've just told me, I probably will.'

'Take your time.'

'Are you planning to spend the night at La Bicoque?'

'I have no option. People wouldn't understand if I went to a hotel, and there are no trains until tomorrow morning.'

'Did you and your mother have an argument?'

'When?'

'This afternoon.'

'We told each other a few home truths, coldly, as usual. It has become almost a game, the moment we are together.'

She hadn't eaten a dessert and, before leaving the table, she applied her lipstick, looking at herself in a little mirror, and shook a tiny powder puff.

Her eyes were extraordinarily light, a clearer blue even than Valentine's, but as empty as the sky earlier when Maigret had hoped to see the green ray.

4. *The Cliff Path*

Maigret was wondering whether the end of the meal would also be the end of their conversation or whether they would continue it elsewhere, and Arlette was busy lighting a cigarette, when the owner came over to Maigret and spoke to him in an exaggeratedly hushed voice, so softly that Maigret had to ask him to repeat what he had said.

'You're wanted on the telephone.'

'Who?'

The manager gave a meaningful look in the direction of the young woman and the two of them misunderstood each other. Arlette's features hardened, without losing their impassive expression.

'Would you kindly tell me who is asking to speak to me?' said Maigret impatiently.

And the man replied, annoyed, as if being forced to reveal a state secret:

'Monsieur Charles Besson.'

Maigret smiled furtively at Arlette, who must have thought that it was her husband, and rose, saying:

'Will you wait for me?'

She fluttered her eyelashes to indicate that she would, and he walked over to the booth, accompanied by the manager who muttered:

'I should have handed you a note, shouldn't I? I must apologize on behalf of one of my staff. Apparently Monsieur Besson called you two or three times during the day, but no one told you when you came back for dinner.'

A booming voice on the other end of the phone, one of those voices that make the receiver vibrate.

'Detective Chief Inspector Maigret? I'm very sorry, truly. I don't know how to ask for your forgiveness, but perhaps you won't be too annoyed with me when I tell you what happened.'

Maigret couldn't get a word in edgeways. The voice went on:

'I drag you away from your work, from your family. I make you come to Étretat and I'm not even here to welcome you. I must tell you that I intended to be at the station this morning, that I desperately tried to contact the stationmaster to give him a message for you. Hello! . . .'

'Yes.'

'Would you believe that last night I had to rush off to Dieppe where my wife's mother was at death's door.'

'Did she die?'

'Not until this afternoon and, since she only has daughters and I was the only man in the house, I had to stay. You know how it is. You have to think of everything. There are unforeseen circumstances. I couldn't telephone you from the house because my dying mother-in-law couldn't stand the slightest sound, but I managed to get away for a few minutes three times to call you from a nearby bar. It was awful.'

'Was she in a great deal of pain?'

'Not particularly, but she knew she was dying.'

'How old was she?'

'Eighty-eight. Now I'm back in Fécamp, where I'm looking after the children, because I left my wife in Dieppe. She only has the baby with her. If you wish, I can jump into my car and come and see you this evening. Otherwise tell me what time tomorrow morning. I shan't take up too much of your time and I'll make it my duty to be there.'

'Is there something you'd like to tell me?'

'You mean to do with what happened on Sunday?

'I know no more than what you've been told. Oh! I did want to let you know that I've managed to get hold of all the Normandy newspapers, both from Le Havre and Rouen. None of them mentions the case, which means the Paris papers won't either. That was no easy task. I had to go to Rouen in person on Tuesday morning. They printed three lines about it, saying it is presumed to be an accident.'

He stopped for breath at long last, but Maigret had nothing to say.

'Are you comfortably settled? Have they given you a good room? I hope you'll shed some light on this distressing affair. I don't know if you're an early riser. Shall I be at your hotel at nine o'clock?'

'If that's convenient.'

'Thank you, and once again I apologize.'

When Maigret came out of the booth he caught a glimpse of Arlette, who had remained alone in the dining room, her elbows on the table, while the staff were clearing away.

'He had to go to Dieppe,' he said.

'Has she finally croaked?'

'Was she ill?'

'She's been saying she's dying for twenty or thirty years. Charles must be delighted.'

'Did he not like her?'

'He's going to be all right for a good while, because there's a huge inheritance. Do you know Dieppe?'

'Not well.'

'The Montets own around a quarter of all the houses in the city. He's going to be rich, but he'll manage to lose all that money in some outlandish enterprise. Unless Mimi stops him, it's her money after all, and I think she's capable of standing up to him.'

It was strange: she said all this without animosity; there was no spitefulness in her voice, no envy; she sounded as though she was simply talking about people as she saw them and they appeared in a harsher light than in the photos of the Criminal Records department.

Maigret had sat back down opposite her and filled his pipe, which he hesitated to light.

'Tell me when I start to get on your nerves.'

'You don't seem in a hurry to go back to La Bicoque.'

'I'm not.'

'To the extent that you prefer any old company?'

He knew that this was not true, that now she had begun to talk about herself, she probably wanted to say more. But most of the lights had now been turned off in the vast dining room and the staff were signalling that they had outstayed their welcome, making it difficult to pick up the conversation where they had left off.

'Would you like to go somewhere else?'

'Where? If we go to a bar we might bump into Théo, and I'd rather avoid him.'

'Do you still love him?'

'No. I don't know.'

'Are you angry with him?'

'I don't know. Come on. We can always go for a walk.'

The night was dark and the fog created broad halos around the few electric streetlights. The regular crashing of the waves was much louder than during the day, making quite a din.

'May I carry on asking you questions?'

She was wearing very high heels and he was careful to avoid the streets that had no pavements, especially the ones with big, uneven cobblestones which might trip her up.

'That's why I'm here. You'll have to ask them sooner or later, won't you? I'd like to go back to Paris tomorrow with my mind at rest.'

It was many years since Maigret had had the occasion to wander around at night through the dark, cold streets of a small town in the company of a pretty woman, and he felt almost guilty. There were few people out and about. Their footsteps could be heard long before they loomed out of the darkness. Most of them turned round to look at this nocturnal couple, and perhaps people were spying on them from behind the curtains of the lit windows too.

'Sunday was your mother's birthday, I gather.'

'The third of September, yes. My stepfather turned

that date into something as important as a national holiday and would not hear of any member of the family missing it. We've kept up the habit of getting together at my mother's on that date. It's become a tradition, do you understand?'

'Except for Théo, from what you told me earlier.'

'Except for Théo, since his father's death.'

'Did you bring presents? May I ask what?'

'Funnily enough, Mimi and I brought almost the same gift: a lace collar. It's hard to find presents for my mother, who's had everything she ever wanted, the rarest and most expensive things. When you give her a trinket, she bursts out laughing in a hurtful way and thanks you over-effusively. Since she loves lace, we both had the same idea.'

'No chocolates, sweets or cakes?'

'I can guess what you're thinking. No. It wouldn't occur to anyone to give her chocolates or sweets, which she hates. You see, Mother is one of those women who look frail and delicate but who prefer a grilled or pickled herring, a jar of gherkins or a nice piece of salted pork to cakes or sweets.'

'What about you?'

'No.'

'Has anyone in the family ever suspected what happened in the past between you and your stepfather?'

'To be honest, I'm not sure, but I'd swear that Mother was always aware of it.'

'Who'd have told her?'

'She doesn't need anyone. I'm sorry to speak ill of her

again, but she's always listened at keyholes. It's an obsession. She spied on me before spying on Ferdinand. She spied on everyone in the house, in *her* house, including the butler, the driver and the maids.'

'Why?'

'Because she wanted to know. Because it was *her house*.'

'And do you think she knew about Théo as well?'

'I'm almost certain.'

'Did she ever say anything to you or make any allusion to it? You weren't even twenty, were you? She could have warned you.'

'Why would she do that?'

'When you announced your intention to marry Julien Sudre, didn't she try to dissuade you? In other words, in those days it could have been considered a poor match. Ferdinand Besson was at the height of his career. You lived a life of luxury and you were marrying a penniless dentist with no prospects.'

'Mother didn't say anything.'

'What about your stepfather?'

'He didn't dare. He felt awkward about me. I think he regretted his behaviour. Deep down, I think he was a very honest man, scrupulous even. He must have been convinced that I was doing it because of him. He wanted to give me a big dowry, which Julien turned down.'

'At your request?'

'Yes.'

'Your mother never suspected anything?'

'No.'

Now they were on a path that led to the top of the cliff; at regular intervals they could see the Antifer beacon sweeping the sky, and they could hear the mournful wail of the foghorn in the darkness. The pungent smell of wrack reached their nostrils. Arlette showed no sign of tiredness and didn't complain of the cold, despite her high heels and her Parisian outfit.

'I'm going to ask a few more personal questions.'

'I'm prepared for nearly all of the questions you're asking me.'

'When did you find out that you couldn't have children? Before getting married?'

'Yes.'

'How?'

'Have you forgotten what I told you earlier?'

'I haven't forgotten but—'

'No, I didn't take any precautions whatsoever and I didn't allow the men to take any.'

'Why not?'

'I don't know. Perhaps out of a sort of integrity.'

He had the feeling she was blushing in the dark, and that there was something different in her voice.

'How did you know for certain?'

'Through a young houseman at Lariboisière hospital.'

'Who was your lover?'

'Like the rest. He examined me and had me examined by his friends.'

He hesitated, embarrassed by the question that sprang to his lips. She sensed it.

'Say it! I've got nothing left to lose . . .'

'This appointment with his friends, was it strictly for medical purposes or—'

'*Or* . . . yes!'

'Now I understand.'

'That I needed to put a stop to all that, right?'

She still spoke with the same sang-froid, in a detached tone, as if this weren't about her but about a pathological case.

'Ask the other question.'

'My goodness, yes. During these . . . amorous adventures, and later, with your husband or with others, did you ever feel—'

'Normal pleasure? Is that what you mean?'

'I was going to say "satisfaction".'

'Neither. You're not the first person to ask me that, you know. Although I sometimes follow a man in the street, I also sleep with intelligent men and even men of great standing.'

'Is Hervé Peyrot one of them?'

'He's a conceited idiot.'

'How would you react if your mother suddenly told you that she knew about that side of your life?'

'I'd tell her to mind her own business.'

'Supposing that, in the belief that it was her duty, and in the hope of saving you, she were to inform you that she was going to tell your husband about it?'

A silence. She had stopped walking.

'Is that what you're leading up to?' she asked reproachfully.

'Not intentionally.'

'I don't know. I told you that I wouldn't want Julien to find out for anything in the world.'

'Why?'

'Haven't you understood?'

'Because you're afraid of hurting him?'

'Partly. Julien is happy. He's one of the happiest men I know. No one has the right to take away his joy. And besides . . .'

'Besides?'

'He's probably the only man who respects me, who treats me other than . . . than you know what.'

'And you need that?'

'Maybe.'

'So that if your mother—'

'If she threatened to sully me in his eyes, I would do anything to stop her.'

'Including killing her?'

'Yes.'

She added:

'I can assure you that the situation has not yet occurred.'

'Why do you say *not yet*?'

'Because now not only does she know, but she has proof. She spoke to me about Hervé this afternoon.'

'What did she say?'

'You'd probably be surprised if I told you what she said. You see, despite her airs and graces, Mother has remained very working class, very much the fisherman's daughter, and in private she can be quite foul-mouthed. She told me I could have been content with playing the whore elsewhere than under her roof, using the filthiest language to refer to what happened between Hervé and me. She was just as rude about Julien, calling him a pimp, because she's convinced he knows about it and takes advantage.'

'Did you defend him?'

'I ordered my mother to shut up.'

'How?'

'By looking her in the eyes and telling her that I *wanted* her to shut up. Since she wouldn't I slapped her, and she was so taken aback that she stopped at once.'

'Is she waiting for you?'

'I'm sure she won't go to bed until I'm back.'

'Do you really want to go and sleep at her house?'

'You know the situation, and you must admit that I don't really have any choice. Before I leave I have to be certain that she won't say anything to Julien, that she won't do anything that might worry him.'

After a silence, sensing Maigret's anxiety perhaps, she gave a wry little laugh.

'Don't worry. There won't be a murder!'

They had reached the top of the cliff and a milky fog obscured their view of the sea, which could be heard pounding the rocks.

'We can take the path on the right back down. It's better and brings us out almost opposite La Bicoque. Are you sure you don't have any more questions for me?'

The moon must have risen above the mist, which was now faintly incandescent, and, when Arlette stopped, he saw the pale shape of her face, with the wide line of her mouth.

'Not for the time being,' he replied.

Then, still standing there in front of him, she said in a changed voice, which was painful to hear:

'And . . . don't you want to take advantage of me, like the others?'

He nearly reacted to her the way she had reacted to her mother earlier that day, by slapping her as if she was a naughty little girl. But he merely gripped her arm hard and forced her to start making her way down the cliff path.

'Mind you, what I was saying was for your benefit.'

'Shut up!'

'Admit you're tempted.'

He squeezed her arm harder, deliberately hurting her.

'Are you sure you won't regret saying no?'

Her voice had become shriller, sounding cruel and sarcastic.

'Think carefully, inspector!'

He abruptly let go of her arm, filled his pipe and continued down the cliff, taking no further notice of her. He heard her stop again, then continue slowly and finally hasten her steps to catch up with him.

Maigret's face was illuminated by the glow from the match he was holding over the bowl of his pipe.

'I'm sorry. I behaved like an idiot just now.'

'Yes.'

'Are you very angry with me?'

'Let's not mention it any more.'

'Did you really think I wanted to?'

'No.'

'What I wanted, after having been forced to humiliate myself as I did, was to hurt you back, to humiliate you.'

'I know.'

'I'd have felt avenged, watching you lying on top of me like an animal.'

'Come on.'

'Admit that you believe I tried to kill my mother.'

'Not yet.'

'Do you mean that you're not sure?'

'I simply mean what I said; in other words, that I have no idea.'

'When you think I'm guilty, will you tell me?'

'Probably.'

'Will you tell me to my face?'

'I promise.'

'But I'm not guilty.'

'I hope not.'

He'd had enough now of this strained conversation. Arlette's insistence annoyed him. She seemed to derive too much satisfaction from analysing and denigrating herself.

'Mother isn't in bed yet.'

'How do you know?'

'The little light you can see is the sitting-room lamp.'

'What time is your train tomorrow?'

'I'd like to get the eight o'clock one. Unless you want me to stay here. In that case I'll telephone Julien and tell him that Mother needs me.'

'Does he know you hate your mother?'

'I don't hate her. I just don't love her, that's all. Can I take the eight o'clock train?'

'Yes.'

'I shan't see you again before I leave?'

'I don't know yet.'

'Perhaps you'd like to go and check that Mother's still alive and well before I go?'

'Perhaps.'

They had just descended a steep slope, a sort of embankment, and they came out on to the road, fifty metres from the gate of La Bicoque.

'Are you coming in?'

'No.'

They couldn't see the windows and could only just make out the light through the thick curtain of shrubs.

'Good night, Monsieur Maigret!'

'Good night!'

She was loath to take her leave of him.

'Are you still angry with me?'

'I don't know. Go to bed!'

And, thrusting his hands in his pockets, he strode off in the direction of the town.

His mind was in turmoil and, now that he'd left her, dozens of questions which he hadn't thought to ask came into his head. He regretted having given her permission to go back to Paris the next morning and was about to retrace his steps and order her to stay.

Perhaps it was a mistake to leave the two women alone together overnight? Might not that afternoon's scene be repeated more heatedly and turn dangerously violent?

He would be delighted to see Valentine again and talk to her, sitting in her tiny living room surrounded by harmless knick-knacks.

At nine o'clock he would meet the blustering Charles Besson, who would deafen him with his loud talk.

Étretat was a ghost town, and the casino was already in darkness for want of customers. At a street corner there was only one bar with its light on, a café rather, which probably stayed open in the winter for the locals.

Maigret paused on the pavement outside, because he was thirsty. In the yellowish light inside, he glimpsed the now familiar form of Théo Besson, still looking very much the Englishman in his tweed suit.

He was holding a glass and talking to someone standing beside him, a fairly young man in a black suit, the sort farmers wear on Sundays, with a white shirt and a dark tie, a boy with a very ruddy face and a weather-beaten neck.

Maigret turned the handle and went up to the bar without looking at them and ordered a beer.

Now he could see both of them in the mirror behind the bottles, and he thought he caught Théo giving his companion a look signalling to him to be quiet.

There was a heavy silence in the bar where they were only four people, including the owner, plus a black cat curled up on a chair in front of the stove.

'We've got fog again,' said the owner, at length. 'It's the time of year. It's still sunny during the daytime, though.'

The young man turned round to stare at Maigret, who

was emptying his pipe by banging it against his heel and crushing the hot ashes in the sawdust. There was an arrogance in his eyes, and he reminded Maigret of those village cockerels who, having had a few drinks at a wedding or a funeral, strut around looking for a fight.

'Aren't you the man who came from Paris this morning?' asked the owner, for the sake of talking.

Maigret simply nodded, and the young braggart stared at him all the more intently.

This went on for a few minutes, during which Théo Besson merely gazed morosely at the bottles in front of him. He had the complexion, the eyes, especially the rings under his eyes, of those who drink a lot, regularly, from the moment they wake up. He also had an indifferent look and a rather limp manner.

'Same again!' he ordered.

The owner glanced at the young man, who nodded his assent. So they were together.

Théo downed his glass in one. The other man did likewise and, when the elder Besson had tossed a few notes on to the bar, they both left, not without the young man turning round a couple of times to look at Maigret.

'Who is he?'

'Don't you know him? That's Monsieur Théo, Valentine's stepson.'

'What about the young man?'

'One of the brothers of young Rose, who died when she drank the poison intended for her mistress, poor girl.'

'The eldest brother?'

'Henri, yes. He's a herring fisherman in Fécamp.'

'Did they come in here together?'

'I think so, yes. Wait a sec. When they arrived there were several people at the bar. In any case, if they didn't come in at the same time, it was close.'

'Do you happen to know what they were talking about?'

'No. In the first place it was noisy, with several conversations going on at the same time. Then I went downstairs to tap a new barrel.'

'Have you seen them together before?'

'I don't think so. I'm not sure. But I've seen Monsieur Théo with the young lady.'

'Which young lady?'

'Young Rose.'

'Did you see them in the street?'

'I saw them here, in my bar, at least twice.'

'Was he chasing her?'

'It depends what you mean by chasing. They didn't kiss and he didn't touch her, if that's what you mean. But they were chatting away and laughing, and I could see he was trying to get her drunk. That wasn't difficult with young Rose, she'd start giggling after one glass of wine and was sozzled after the second.'

'How long ago was that?'

'Just a moment. The last time was around a week ago. I know! It was Wednesday, because it was the day my wife went to Le Havre, and she goes there every Wednesday.'

'When was the first time?'

'Maybe a week or two before that.'

'Is Monsieur Théo a good customer?'

'He's not a particular customer of mine. He's the

customer of anywhere serving drinks. He has nothing to do all day, so he wanders around. Only he can't see an open café or bar without popping inside. He's never noisy; he never picks a fight with anyone. Sometimes, at night, he lisps and finds it difficult to get certain words out, but that's all.'

Suddenly, the owner looked as if he regretted being so forthcoming.

'I hope you don't suspect him of trying to poison his stepmother? If there's one person I'd trust, it's him. Besides, people who drink the way he does are never dangerous. The worst are those who get drunk occasionally and don't know what they're doing any more.'

'Have you seen Rose's brother often?'

'Rarely. People from Yport don't like coming to Étretat. They're a special breed. They prefer to go to Fécamp, which is close by, and where they feel more at home. A little Calvados, to help the beer down? It's my round.'

'No. Another beer.'

The beer was not good, and it lay on Maigret's stomach for a long time. He kept waking suddenly and had nightmares, which he couldn't even remember, but which left him with a feeling of despondency. When he finally got up, the mournful wail of the foghorn could be heard, and the tide must have been high because the hotel shuddered each time a wave pounded the shore.

5. The Opinions of a Good Man

The fog had almost entirely dispersed, but a haze still hung over the calm sea that swelled gently with a slow breathing motion and rainbows shone in the fine mist.

The town's houses began to turn golden in the fresh sunlight, and the air was cool, a delicious coolness that tingled through every pore. The vegetable stalls smelled good, bottles of milk stood on the doorsteps and it was the hour when the bakeries were filled with warm, crisp bread.

Once again, the scene conjured up a childhood memory, an image of an idyllic world, an imaginary world. Étretat looked pure and innocent with its houses that were too small, too picturesque, too freshly painted to be the scene of a tragedy, and the cliffs emerged from the mist exactly as they did on the postcards displayed by the door of the general store; the butcher, the baker and the greengrocer could have been characters in a children's storybook.

Was it just Maigret? Or did other people feel the same nostalgia without admitting it? He so wished the world could be the one he had known as a child. In his mind, he said: 'Like a picture postcard.'

It wasn't only the streets and the buildings, but also the people – the father, the mother, the well-behaved children, the kindly white-haired grandparents, and so on.

There had been an entire period, for example, in his early days in the police, when Le Vésinet had seemed to him to be the most peaceful place in the world. It was just outside Paris, but before 1914 there were hardly any motor cars. The wealthy bourgeois still had their country homes in Le Vésinet – big, comfortable brick houses surrounded by well-maintained gardens with fountains, swings and large silver-painted spheres. The menservants wore yellow-striped waistcoats and the maids white caps and lace-trimmed aprons.

Seemingly happy, virtuous families lived in them, families for whom all was peace and joy, and he had been secretly disappointed when an unsavoury business had broken out in one such house with its raked paths – the sordid murder of a stepmother for financial gain.

Now, of course, he knew. He spent his life, in a way, seeing the other side of the coin, but he still had a childlike hankering for a world 'like in the picture postcards'.

The little station was pretty, a watercolour painting by a talented student, with a rose-coloured puff of smoke above its chimney. He saw the toy train, the man who punched the tickets – as a child he had dreamed one day of punching railway tickets – and he saw Arlette arrive, as slim and elegant as the previous day in her Parisian outfit, carrying a crocodile holdall.

Earlier he had almost gone to meet her on the dusty path that must be fragrant with the smell of the hedgerows and tall wild flowers, but he was afraid it would look as if he were hurrying to an assignation. Descending the path with tiny steps in her high heels, she must look very much the 'young mistress of the chateau'.

Why is the reality always so different? Or rather, why do we give children the illusion of a world that doesn't exist and which all their lives they will compare with the harsh reality?

She spotted him immediately, waiting for her on the platform by the newspaper kiosk, and she smiled wearily at him as she handed over her ticket to be punched. She seemed tired and slightly anxious.

'I thought you'd be here,' she said.

'How did it go?'

'It was difficult.'

She looked to see where her compartment was, because there was no corridor on the train. There was only one first-class carriage, and she had it all to herself.

'How about your mother?'

'She's alive. In any case, she was when I left.'

They only had a few moments before the train left and, having put her bag down on the seat, she stood by the door.

'Did you have another argument?'

'We stayed up half the night. There's something I have to say to you, Monsieur Maigret. It's only a feeling, but it bothers me. Rose is dead, but my instinct tells me that it isn't over, that there's going to be another tragedy.'

'Because of what your mother said to you?'

'No. I don't know why.'

'Do you think she's still in danger?'

She did not reply. Her blue eyes gazed in the direction of the kiosk.

'The inspector's over there, waiting for you,' she said, as if the spell was broken.

And she stepped on to the train as the stationmaster raised his whistle to his lips and the engine began to belch out steam.

And so the inspector was. He had arrived earlier than anticipated, and, finding that Maigret wasn't at his hotel, had come to the station searching for him. It was slightly embarrassing. Now why was that?

The train slowly pulled out of the station, then stopped with a great shudder after a few metres while Maigret was shaking hands with Castaing.

'Any news?'

'Nothing special,' replied Castaing. 'But I was worried, for no particular reason. I dreamed about the two women, the mother and the daughter, alone in that little house.'

'Which one killed the other?'

Now it was Castaing's turn to feel awkward.

'How do you know? In my dream it was the mother who killed the daughter. And guess what she used? A log from the fireplace!'

'Charles Besson should be here at nine o'clock. His mother-in-law died. Has Lucas telephoned yet with some information?'

'There isn't much, but he'll call back when he has more, and I left instructions at the station to contact us at your hotel when he does.'

'Nothing on Théo?'

'He's had a spot of bother a few times over cheques that bounced. He's always paid up before being taken to court. Most of his friends are wealthy. They like to party and be surrounded by people. He does the occasional business deal, mainly acting as go-between.'

'No women?'

'He doesn't seem particularly interested in women. He sometimes has a girlfriend, never for long.'

'Is that all?'

The smell of coffee and *eau de vie* coming from a little café was so tempting that neither of them could resist going inside. They leaned on the bar over a large cup of coffee giving off a whiff of alcohol.

'It's not so much my dream that worried me,' Castaing went on in a hushed voice, 'as a train of thought I had before going to sleep. I even shared it with my wife, because I think better aloud than in my head, and she agreed with me. It's five years now since old Besson – Ferdinand – died, isn't it?'

'About that.'

'And since then, as far as we know, the situation hasn't changed. But it wasn't until last Sunday that someone tried to poison Valentine. And mark you, they chose the only day when there were enough people in the house to divert suspicion.'

'That makes sense. And then?'

'It's not Valentine who died, but poor Rose. So, if someone had a reason to do away with Valentine, the reason still exists. So, until we discover that reason—'

'The threat is still there. Is that what you mean?'

'Yes. Perhaps that threat is more serious than ever, precisely because you're here. Valentine has no fortune. Therefore it wasn't for her money that someone attempted to kill her. Might it be because she knows something that the killer wants to prevent her from revealing? In that case . . .'

Maigret listened to Castaing's reasoning seemingly unimpressed. He gazed out of the window at the delectable morning, the dewy moisture of the night making the sun's rays shimmer.

'Did Lucas say anything about Julien?'

'The Sudres have a comfortable lifestyle, in an affordable rented four-bedroom apartment. They have a maid and a car, and they spend their weekends in the country.'

'I knew that.'

'Hervé Peyrot, the wine merchant, is wealthy. He has large premises on Quai de Bercy and fritters away most of his time with women – all sorts of women. He has three cars, including a Bugatti.'

'Family beach' Maigret had read somewhere in a brochure. And it was true. Mothers with children, husbands who came to join them on Saturday evening; elderly ladies and gentlemen with their bottle of mineral water and box of pills on the table in the hotel dining room, who always sat in the same seats in the casino; the Seuret sisters' patisserie, where people went to eat cakes and ice cream; the old fishermen, always the same, whom visitors photographed posing next to their boats pulled up on the pebble beach.

Ferdinand Besson had been a respectable-looking elderly gentleman too, and Valentine was the most delightful old lady; Arlette, that morning, could have been a model for a picture postcard, her husband was a hardworking dentist, while Théo was the epitome of the gentleman whom people forgive for drinking a bit too much because he is always so quiet and so distinguished.

Now Charles Besson was arriving with his wife and four children, including a baby only a few months old. And while waiting for his mourning clothes to be ready he had sewn a black crepe armband on to his sleeve, because his mother-in-law had died.

He was a deputy, and was already on first-name terms with the minister. During his electoral campaign he must have gone around warmly shaking hands, kissing babies, having a drink with the fishermen and the farmers.

He was also what is generally considered a fine figure of a man – that is how Maigret's mother, for example, would have described him – tall with broad shoulders, slightly plump, paunchy, his eyes almost disingenuous and full lips beneath his moustache.

'I hope I haven't kept you waiting, detective chief inspector? Good morning, Castaing. Delighted to see you again.'

His car had recently had a fresh coat of paint and looked brand new.

'No bad news?'

'Nothing.'

'My stepmother?'

'Seems fine. Arlette has just left.'

'Ah! Did she come back? That was nice of her. I was sure she'd be there to comfort her mother.'

'Would you excuse us for a moment, Monsieur Besson?'

And Maigret took Castaing aside, told him to go to Yport, and on to Fécamp if need be.

'I apologize. I had to give him some instructions. I'm afraid I'm not too sure where we can go to talk. I doubt my room has been cleaned yet.'

'I'll gladly have a drink. After that, if you're not afraid of some fresh air, we can sit on the terrace of the casino. I hope you'll forgive me for not being here to welcome you. My wife is deeply distressed. Her sister has just arrived from Marseille, where she's married to a ship-owner. There are only the two of them now. The Montets didn't have a son and so I'm the one who'll have to deal with all the complications.'

'Are you expecting any complications?'

'I shan't speak ill of my mother-in-law Montet. She was a good woman, but she had her neuroses, especially as she grew older. Has anyone told you that her husband had a construction company? He built half the houses in Dieppe as well as numerous public buildings. Most of the fortune he left is in property. My mother-in-law ran things herself after her husband's death. But she would never agree to carry out repairs. Hence a huge number of lawsuits with tenants, the town council and even with the tax authorities.'

'One question, Monsieur Besson. Did your mother-in-law and Valentine see each other?'

Maigret drank another coffee laced with alcohol as he

watched Charles Besson, who at close quarters seemed weaker, more lacking in character.

'Sadly they didn't. They always refused to meet.'

'Both of them?'

'That's to say that it was my wife's mother who refused to have anything to do with Valentine. It's a ridiculous business. When I introduced Mimi to her, Valentine looked closely at her hands and said something like: "You probably have your father's hands, don't you?"

'"Why?"

'"Because I suppose that a builder's hands must be bigger and broader than average."

'It's ridiculous, you see! True, my father-in-law started out as a builder, but he wasn't one for long. Even so, he remained rather foul-mouthed. I think he did it on purpose, because he was very rich; he became an important figure in Dieppe and the entire region, and he enjoyed shocking people with his dress and his language.

'My mother-in-law retorted in the same vein. "It's better than being the daughter of a fisherman who drank himself to death!"

'Then she reminded Valentine that she'd been a sales assistant at the Seuret sisters' patisserie.'

'Accusing her of not behaving in an exemplary manner?'

'Yes. She pointed out the age difference between Valentine and her husband. In short, they always refused to speak to one another.'

He added with a shrug:

'All families have a similar story, don't they? But all the same, they're both good women in their own way.'

'Are you very fond of Valentine?'

'Very. She's always been very kind to me.'

'What about your wife?'

'Mimi is less taken with her, naturally.'

'Do they argue?'

'They don't see each other very often, once a year on average. Before coming I always advise Mimi to be patient, reminding her that Valentine is elderly. She promises, but there's always a bittersweet exchange of words.'

'Last Sunday as well?'

'I don't know. I took the children for a walk.'

And speaking of children, what did Charles' children think of their father?

Doubtless, like most children, that he was a strong, clever man, able to protect them and guide them. They couldn't see that he was weak, ill adjusted to reality.

Mimi probably said:

'He's such a kind man!'

Because he loved everybody, watched life unfold with big, innocent, avid eyes. He truly would have liked to be strong, clever and the best of men!

And he had his ideas, he was bursting with ideas. If he didn't pull them all off, and if, when he did, they ended up in disaster, it was because life was against him.

But he'd managed to get himself elected deputy, hadn't he? Now he would be recognized for the man he was. The entire country would know his name; he would be made minister, become a great statesman.

'When you were young, were you ever in love with Valentine? After all, she was barely ten years older than you.'

He looked offended, indignant.

'Absolutely no way!'

'And later, were you not in love with Arlette?'

'I always thought of her as a sister.'

He still saw the world and men as if in a picture. He took a cigar from his pocket, surprised that Maigret didn't smoke one too, lit it carefully, meticulously, and slowly drew in the smoke, which he then exhaled, and watched as it rose into the golden air.

'Shall we go and sit on the terrace? There are comfortable armchairs overlooking the beach. We'll be able to see the sea.'

He lived by the sea all year round, but he always derived the same pleasure from watching it, ensconced in a comfortable chair – well dressed, clean shaven, with all the airs of an important, prosperous man.

'What about your brother Théo?'

'Are you asking me if he was in love with Valentine?'

'Yes.'

'Absolutely not. I never noticed anything of the kind.'

'And with Arlette?'

'Even less. I was still a kid when Théo was already having affairs, especially with what I call "women of easy virtue".'

'Wasn't Arlette in love with him either?'

'Perhaps she had a crush on him, as my wife would say when talking about little girls' infatuations. You know how it is. Nothing of any consequence. The proof being that she soon got married.'

'Were you not surprised?'

'About what?'

'About her marriage to Julien Sudre.'

'No. Perhaps a little, because he wasn't rich and we thought that Arlette would find it hard to live without luxuries. There was a time when she was quite a snob. She got over it. I think she really fell in love with Julien. He was very noble. My father wanted to give Arlette a generous dowry, because in those days we were very well-off, and he said no.'

'Arlette too?'

'Yes. So overnight she had to adapt to a modest lifestyle. As we did, but later on.'

'Do your wife and Arlette get on well?'

'I think so. Even though they are very different. Mimi has children, a whole household to run. She rarely goes out.'

'Wouldn't she like to go out? Has she never wanted to live in Paris?'

'She hates Paris.'

'Doesn't she miss Dieppe either?'

'Maybe a little. Unfortunately, now that I'm a deputy we can't go and live there. My constituents wouldn't understand.'

Charles Besson's words were perfectly in keeping with the surroundings, with the picture-postcard blue sea, the dazzling white cliffs and the bathers filing down to the beach as if for a photograph.

Ultimately, did all this really exist or was it make-believe? Was it this smug, paunchy fellow who was right?

Was young Rose dead, or not?

'Were you not surprised, last Sunday, to find your brother here?'

'A little, at first. I thought he was in Deauville, or rather, as it's now September and the hunting season has begun, in some chateau in Sologne. Théo, you know, continues to move in society circles. When he still had a fortune, he lived extravagantly and was very generous to his friends. They haven't forgotten, and now he's their guest.'

This put things in a new light! A few words and they were no longer talking about the same Théo.

'Does he have any means?'

'Financial means? I don't know. Very few if he does have any. But he has no outgoings. He's unmarried.'

A hint of envy, all the same, in the voice of the big man burdened with his four kids.

'He's always very elegant, but that's because his clothes last him a long time. He's often invited by his high-society friends. I think he dabbles in the occasional business deal. He's a very clever fellow, you know, and had he wanted to . . .'

Charles too, no doubt, had he wanted to . . .

'Did he agree to go to Valentine's with you straight away?'

'No, not straight away.'

'Did he tell you why he was here?'

'I hope, inspector, that you don't suspect Théo?'

'I suspect no one, Monsieur Besson. We are simply having a chat. I am trying to piece together as accurate a picture of the family as I can.'

'Well, if you want my opinion, Théo is a sentimentalist,

although he'd never admit it. He felt nostalgic for Étretat, where we used to spend our holidays when we were children. Do you know that we used to come here when my mother was alive?'

'I understand.'

'I pointed out to him that there was no reason to remain on bad terms with Valentine and that she didn't hold a grudge against him either. In the end he came back to the house with me.'

'How did he behave?'

'Like a man of the world. A bit awkward at first. When he saw our gifts, he apologized for having come empty-handed.'

'And towards Arlette?'

'What? There was never anything between him and Arlette.'

'So when you sat down to dinner, the entire family was there.'

'Except for Sudre, who hadn't been able to come.'

'I'd forgotten. And you didn't notice anything, no little detail that could have made you suspicious?'

'Absolutely nothing. Even though I'm generally quite observant.'

Fool! But how nice it is sometimes to be a fool!

'I have to say that Mimi and I were pretty busy with the children. At home they're relatively quiet. But when we take them out, they get over-excited. You've seen how tiny Valentine's house is. The dining room was so full that you couldn't turn around. The baby, who normally sleeps most of the time, screamed for over an hour, and it was driving us all mad. We had to put the little one to sleep in my stepmother's bed, and we didn't know what to do with the older ones.'

'Did you know young Rose well?'

'I saw her every time I came to La Bicoque. She seemed like a good girl, a little taciturn, like a lot of the folk around here. But once you got to know her—'

'So in all you'd met her half a dozen times?'

'A little more.'

'Did you ever have a conversation with her?'

'As one does with a servant, about the weather, about food. She was a good cook and Valentine enjoyed her food. I wonder what she's going to do now. You see, inspector, as I listen to you and answer your questions, I'm a little worried that you're on the wrong track.'

Maigret remained impassive, gently puffing on his pipe as he watched a tiny ship moving imperceptibly across the curve of the horizon.

'In fact it's because I foresaw it, I mean I foresaw the direction the police investigation would take, that I contacted the minister and asked him to do me the kindness of putting you in charge of the case.'

'Thank you very much.'

'Not at all! Thank *you* for coming.

'Although I have always been a very busy man, I have had the occasion, like everyone else, to read detective novels.

'No need to ask whether I take them seriously. In detective novels everyone has something to hide, everyone has something on their conscience, and you realize that the people who outwardly seem the simplest actually have a complicated life.

'Now that you are acquainted with the family, I'd like to think it's clear that none of us had any reason to resent my stepmother, especially not enough to think of killing her in cold blood.

'Arsenic was found in Rose's stomach, and it seems to me that there was no doubt, if I understand correctly, that it was in the glass containing Valentine's medicine.

'I'm not arguing with the experts' findings, I'm sure they know what they're doing, even though they have often been known to get things wrong and even to argue among themselves.

'You've met Arlette. You've glimpsed Théo from a distance. You're seeing me. As for Mimi, were it not for the unfortunate circumstances that have befallen her, I'd have brought her with me and you would have seen that she wouldn't hurt a fly.

'We were all happy on Sunday. And I would go so far as to say, even if people laugh at me, that the tragedy could only have been an accident.

'Do you believe in ghosts?'

Besson was delighted with his surprise question, which he threw out with a knowing smile, in the same way that he'd have tripped up a political adversary.

'I don't.'

'Neither do I. All the same, every year there are reports of a haunted house somewhere or other in France and for days, sometimes weeks, the entire population is in a frenzy. In one village in my constituency I've seen all the local gendarmes and police called out, as well as experts, who could find no reason why certain pieces of furniture moved each night. But eventually an explanation emerges, usually one that's so simple that everyone ends up laughing about it.'

'Rose is dead, isn't she?'

'I know. I shan't go so far as to suggest that she could have poisoned herself.'

'Doctor Jolly, who was her general practitioner, states that she was sound in body and mind. There is nothing, in her relations or in her life, to suggest that she wanted to commit suicide. Don't forget that the poison was in the glass when Valentine wanted to take her medicine, because she found it too bitter and didn't drink it.'

'Agreed. I'm not implying anything. I am simply saying this: no one present had anything to gain from killing a harmless old lady.'

'Are you aware that there was a man in the house that night?'

He turned slightly red and made a dismissive gesture as if to brush away a tiresome fly.

'So I've been told. I found it hard to believe. But, after all, Arlette is thirty-eight. She's extraordinarily beautiful and is subjected to more temptations than others. Perhaps it's not as serious as we think? I hope, in any case, that Julien never finds out.'

'He probably never will.'

'You see, Monsieur Maigret, casting suspicion on those who were present is what anyone would have done. But you're different. From what I know, you'll dig deep; you'll go beyond surface appearances and I am convinced that, as with the ghosts, you'll discover a perfectly simple truth.'

'That Rose isn't dead, for example?'

Charles Besson laughed, a little uncertain, however, as to whether Maigret was joking.

'And anyway, how does a person get hold of arsenic? In what form?'

'Don't forget that your father was a pharmacist, that Théo, from what I've been told, studied chemistry, that you yourself once worked in a laboratory – in other words, everyone in the family has some pharmaceutical knowledge.'

'That hadn't occurred to me, but it doesn't change anything as far as I'm concerned.'

'Of course not.'

'Nor does it mean that it couldn't have been an outsider.'

'A vagrant, for example?'

'Why not?'

'Someone who would have waited until the house was full of people to break in through an upstairs window and pour poison into a glass? Because that's also an important aspect of the question. The poison wasn't put into the bottle of medicine, in which no traces were found, but into the glass.'

'You can see it makes no sense!'

'Young Rose is dead.'

'So, what do you think? Tell me your opinion, man to man. I promise you of course that I shan't do anything or repeat anything that might hamper your investigation. Who?'

'I don't know.'

'Why?'

'I don't know yet.'

'How?'

'We'll find out when I've answered the first two questions.'

'Do you have any suspicions?'

He was uncomfortable now, in his armchair, chewing on the end of his cigar, which had gone out and must have tasted acrid. Perhaps, as happened to Maigret, he was clinging to his illusions, to his idea of life which was being shattered. He was an almost pathetic sight, anxious, churned up, watching Maigret's face for the slightest indication.

'Someone killed,' said Maigret.

'There seems to be no doubt about that.'

'People don't kill without a reason, especially when using poison, which means that it couldn't have been a sudden act of anger or passion. During the course of my career I have not seen a single poisoning that was not committed by someone who had something to gain.'

'But who on earth would've had anything to gain, for goodness sake?'

Now he was becoming heated.

'That I don't know yet.'

'Everything my stepmother owns is on an annuity, apart from a few pieces of furniture and knick-knacks.'

'I know.'

'I don't need money, especially at the moment. Neither does Arlette. And Théo doesn't care about money.'

'So I've been told several times.'

'So?'

'So, nothing. I'm only at the start of my investigation, Monsieur Besson. You asked for me and I've come. Valentine also asked me to handle the case.'

'Did she write to you?'

'Neither wrote nor telephoned. She came to see me in Paris.'

'I knew she'd gone to Paris, but I thought it was to visit her daughter.'

'She came to the Police Judiciaire and was in my office while I was receiving a briefing from the minister.'

'That's strange.'

'Why?'

'Because I wouldn't have expected her to have heard of you.'

'She told me that she followed most of my cases in the newspapers and that she had cut out some articles. What's bothering you?'

'Nothing.'

'You prefer not to say?'

'Nothing particular, I assure you, except that I have never known my stepmother to read a newspaper. She doesn't subscribe to any, has always refused to have a wireless and doesn't even have a telephone. She has no interest in what is happening elsewhere.'

'You see how life is full of surprises.'

'Where does this get us?'

'We'll find out later. Perhaps nowhere. Are you thirsty?'

'Is Théo still in Étretat?'

'I spotted him again last night.'

'In that case, we're likely to find him in the bar. Have you talked to him?'

'I haven't had the opportunity.'

'I'll introduce you.'

It was clear that something was needling him and this time he bit off the end of his cigar and lit it distractedly.

Some youths were playing with a big red ball in the surf.

6. *Young Rose and her Problems*

Besson had been right. There was only one person in the bar other than Charlie, who was bustling around getting ready to open up, and that was Théo, playing poker dice on his own, for want of a partner.

Charles walked in, proud and happy to introduce his older brother, and Théo watched him with vacant eyes, reluctantly clambering down from his stool.

'Do you know Detective Chief Inspector Maigret?'

Théo could have said 'only by reputation', or 'as everyone does', anything that would have suggested he knew that Maigret was not just anybody, but he merely inclined his upper body in a very formal manner, without proffering his hand, and mumbled:

'Pleased to meet you.'

Close up, he looked older because the fine lines on his face looked like cracks. He must spend a long time at the barber's each morning having complicated treatments, probably a facial massage, because he had the skin of an old dandy.

'You probably know that Inspector Maigret has agreed to take charge of the investigation, at my request and that of Valentine, who made a special trip to Paris?'

Charles was a little disappointed to see his brother greet him with the polite disdain of a sovereign on a royal visit.

'Are we disturbing you?'

'Not at all.'

'We've just spent an hour in the sun on the beach, and we're thirsty. Charlie!'

The owner gave Maigret a friendly wink.

'What are you drinking, Théo?'

'Scotch.'

'I hate whisky. What will you have, inspector? I'll have a picon-grenadine.'

Why did Maigret have the same? He hadn't had one for a long time and, for some strange reason, the bitter orange liqueur reminded him of his holidays.

'Have you seen Valentine again, since Sunday?'

'No.'

Théo had large, pale, well-manicured hands, with red hairs and a chunky signet ring. He was not wearing a single item of clothing that could be found in an ordinary shop. He had clearly created his own signature style. Someone had made an impression on him, probably an English aristocrat, and he had studied his mannerisms, his walk, his way of dressing and even his facial expressions. From time to time he would casually raise his hand to his mouth as if he were about to yawn, but he didn't.

'Will you be staying much longer in Étretat?'

'I don't know.'

Charles tried hard to make his brother look good, explaining to Maigret:

'He's a strange fellow. He never knows what he'll be doing the following day. For no reason, on a whim, coming out of Fouquet's or Maxim's, he goes home, packs his bags and takes the plane to Cannes or Chamonix, London or Brussels. Don't you, Théo?'

Then Maigret attacked directly:

'May I ask you a question, Monsieur Besson? When did you arrange to see Rose for the last time?'

Poor Charles stared at the two of them in astonishment, opened his mouth as if to protest, and looked as if he was expecting a vehement denial from his elder brother.

But Théo did not deny it. He seemed troubled, and stared into the bottom of his glass for a moment before looking up at Maigret.

'Do you want an exact date?'

'As exact as possible.'

'Charles will tell you that I never know what the date is and that I often don't even know what day of the week it is.'

'Is it more than a week?'

'About a week.'

'Was it a Sunday?'

'No. If I were under oath I would think carefully, but off the top of my head I'd say it was last Wednesday or Thursday.'

'Did you see one another often?'

'I don't know, to be honest. Two or three times.'

'Did you visit her at your stepmother's?'

'You must have been told that I wasn't on speaking terms with my stepmother. When I met the girl, I didn't know where she worked.'

'Where was that?'

'At the Vaucottes fair.'

'Have you started running after servant girls now?' teased Charles, to show that this was not a habit of his older brother's.

'I was watching the sack race. She was next to me and I don't know who spoke first. In any case, she commented that these village fairs were all the same, and that they were stupid and she'd rather go home. Since I was about to leave myself I offered her a lift in my car out of politeness.'

'Is that all?'

'The same again, Charlie!'

The owner refilled the three glasses at once, and Maigret didn't think to object.

'She told me she was an avid reader and she talked about the books she read, the ones she couldn't understand and which troubled her. Should I consider this as an interrogation, inspector? Mind you, I'd be only too pleased to comply, but given our surroundings . . .'

'Come, Théo!' protested Charles. 'Remember, *I'm* the one who asked Monsieur Maigret to come.'

'You are the first person I've met who appears to know the girl a little, or at least the first to talk about her.'

'What else can I tell you?'

'What you thought of her.'

'A little farm girl who had read too much and who asked odd questions.'

'About what?'

'About everything, about kindness, selfishness, about the relations between people, about the human mind – all sorts of things.'

'About love?'

'She told me that she didn't believe in it and that she would never stoop to giving herself to a man.'

'Even in marriage?'

'She thought that marriage was "filthy and nasty", to use her words.'

'So there was nothing between you?'

'Absolutely nothing.'

'No liberties?'

'She'd take my hand when we were walking or lean her head against my shoulder a little when we went for a drive.'

'Did she ever speak to you of hatred?'

'No. Her pet words were selfishness and pride, which she pronounced with a strong Normandy accent. Charlie!'

'In short,' broke in his brother, 'you found it amusing to study her character?'

But Théo didn't bother to reply.

'Is that all, inspector?'

'Did you already know Henri before Rose's death?'

This time Charles displayed genuine consternation. How did Maigret know so much? He hadn't said a word of any of this to him. Théo's behaviour began to appear less natural, and especially his prolonged stay in Étretat.

'I only knew him by name, because she had told me about her entire family, whom she disliked of course, saying that they didn't understand her.'

'Was it after her death that you met Henri Trochu?'

'He stopped me in the street and asked me if I was the man who'd been going out with his sister, and he sounded as if he wanted to pick a fight. I answered him quietly and he calmed down.'

'Have you seen him again?'

'Last night, actually.'

'Why?'

'Because we ran into each other.'

'Is he angry at your family?'

'He's angry with Valentine in particular.'

'For what reason?'

'That's his business. I presume you can question him the way you are questioning me. Charlie!'

Maigret had just realized who it was that Théo was trying so hard to emulate: it was the Duke of Windsor.

'Two or three more questions, since you have so kindly agreed. Did you ever go and see Rose at La Bicoque?'

'Never.'

'And you never waited for her nearby?'

'She used to come here.'

'Did she get drunk in your company?'

'After a glass or two, she'd become very upset.'

'Did she ever express a wish to die?'

'She was scared stiff of death and when we were in the car she'd beg me to slow down.'

'Was she fond of your stepmother? Was she devoted to her?'

'I don't think that two women who live together all day long can be fond of each other.'

'Do you think they hated each other to death?'

'I didn't say that.'

'By the way,' broke in Charles Besson, 'that reminds me that I must visit Valentine. It wouldn't be very nice of me to have come to Étretat and not drop in and see how she is. Will you come with me, inspector?'

'No, thank you.'

'Are you staying here with my brother?'

'I'm staying here for a little while longer.'

'Do you need me today? Tomorrow I'll be in Dieppe, for the funeral. By the way, Théo, my mother-in-law died.'

'Congratulations.'

Charles left, very red in the face, whether from the aperitifs or because of his brother's behaviour, it was not clear.

'Idiot!' muttered Théo. 'So he dragged you all the way from Paris?'

He shrugged and reached for the dice, as if to convey that he had no more to say. Maigret took his wallet out of his pocket and turned to Charlie, but Théo simply mumbled:

'Put it on my tab.'

On coming out of the casino Maigret spotted Castaing's car and Castaing himself was by the hotel, looking for him.

'Have you got a minute? Shall we have a drink?'

'I'd rather not. I think I've just downed three aperitifs in quick succession and I'd prefer not to have another drink straight away.'

Maigret felt numb. He had suddenly begun to see the case in a rather comic light and even Castaing, with his earnest, busy air, seemed like an amusing character.

'My feeling is that you'd do well to go and sniff around Yport. I've been in Normandy for five years and I thought I knew the people well, but I'm out of my depth with that family.'

'What are they saying?'

'Nothing. Neither yes nor no, neither this nor that. They look at me with suspicion, they don't invite me to sit down, seem impatient for me to leave. Sometimes they exchange little glances as if to say: "Shall we talk to him?", "You decide!", "No, you!"

'Then it's the mother who lets slip something that may mean nothing or may be deeply significant.'

'What sort of thing?'

'For example: "Those people close ranks and not one of them will speak."'

'What else?'

'"They must have had their reasons for stopping my daughter from coming here."'

'Did she not go home to see them any more?'

'Rarely, I gather. Because with them you can interpret things as you like. It's as though words don't have the same meaning as normal. They say something and then immediately retract it. They clearly think that we're here not to find out the truth but to protect "those people" from trouble.

'They don't seem to believe that young Rose's death was a mistake. To hear them talking, she was the one meant to die, not Valentine.

'When the father came in, he did offer me a glass of cider, because I was under his roof, but only after dithering for ages. The son was there, because he's not leaving to go fishing until tonight, and he didn't drink with us.'

'Henri, the eldest?'

'Yes. He didn't open his mouth. I think he was trying to signal to them to keep quiet. Perhaps if I ran into the father in a café in Fécamp he'd be more forthcoming with a few drinks inside him. What about you, what have you been doing?'

'I had a chat with the two Besson brothers, Charles first and then Théo.'

They sat down. There was a bottle of white wine in front of them and Castaing filled the two glasses. Maigret took no notice, and when they left the dining room he was tempted to go and have a nap, with the windows wide open looking out over the sea and the sun streaming in.

Modesty prevented him. That too was a legacy from his childhood, a sense of duty which he zealously took to extremes, the feeling that he never did enough to earn his living, so much so that when he was on holiday, which didn't happen every year – take this year, for example – he felt almost guilty.

'What shall I do?' asked Castaing, surprised to see Maigret drowsy and undecided.

'Whatever you like, son. Delve. I don't know where. Perhaps you could speak to the doctor again?'

'Doctor Jolly?'

'Yes. And to people! Anyone! Whoever you come across. The surviving Seuret sister is probably talkative and must be bored all on her own.'

'Shall I drop you somewhere?'

'No thank you.'

He knew that there was a moment like this to get through in every investigation, and that, as if by chance – or was it rather an instinct that drove him? – almost every time he ended up drinking a little too much.

That was when everything started to 'buzz inside his head', as he described to himself.

In the beginning he knew nothing, only precise facts, as written in the reports. Then he would find himself talking to people he'd never seen, whom he hadn't known the day before, and he looked at them as if looking at photographs in an album.

He had to get to know them as quickly as possible, ask questions, believe or disbelieve their answers, avoid forming an opinion too quickly.

It was the period when people and things were clear but a little distant, still anonymous, impersonal.

Then, at a particular point, for no apparent reason, everything 'started to buzz'. The characters became hazier and at the same time more human, more complicated especially, and it was important to pay attention.

In other words, he began to see them from the inside. Groping, ill at ease, he had the feeling that all that was needed was a little effort for everything to become clear and for the truth to emerge unaided.

His hands in his pockets, his pipe in his mouth, he ambled slowly up the already familiar dusty road, and a detail struck him, a simple detail that might possibly be important. He was used to Paris, where transport was available on every street corner.

How far was it from La Bicoque to the centre of Étretat? Around one kilometre. Valentine didn't have the telephone. She no longer had a car and it was unlikely that she rode a bicycle.

So for the old lady it was an expedition to make contact

with other human beings, and she must spend entire days without seeing anyone. Her closest neighbour was Mademoiselle Seuret, who was nearly ninety, and probably never got up from her armchair.

Did Valentine do her shopping herself? Or had Rose done that?

There were fat, purple blackberries in the hedges, but he didn't stop to pick any, or to break off a twig; sadly he was too old for that. He smiled at the idea. He was also thinking about Charles, about his brother Théo, and promised himself that he would also go and have a glass of cider at the Trochus. Would they offer him one?

He pushed open the green gate and inhaled the heady fragrance of all the flowers and shrubs in the garden. He could hear a regular scratching noise and, rounding a bend in the path, saw an old man hoeing around the rose bushes. This must be Honoré, the gardener, who came to work for Valentine three days a week and was also employed by Mademoiselle Seuret.

The man straightened up to look at the intruder and raised a hand to his brow. It wasn't clear whether it was to greet the visitor or to shield his eyes from the sun.

He was a picture-book gardener, almost hunchbacked from bending over, with small, inquisitive eyes and the wary look of an animal poking its head out of its burrow.

He said nothing, followed Maigret with his gaze, and only when he heard the door open did he resume his rhythmic scratching.

It wasn't Madame Leroy who got up to come and open the door but Valentine herself, who acted as if she were welcoming someone she had known for a long time.

'I had a visitor today,' she announced excitedly. 'Charles came to see me. He sounded disappointed with the way his brother behaved towards you.'

'Did he tell you about our conversation?'

'What conversation? Wait a moment. He talked mainly about old Madame Montet, who's died, which is going to make a huge difference to his circumstances. He's rich now, richer than he's ever been, because that old vixen owned more than sixty houses, not to mention the shares and more than likely a nest egg of gold coins. What will you have?'

'A glass of water, as chilled as possible.'

'On condition that you'll have a little drink with it. For me. I never drink alone. That would be terrible, wouldn't it? Can you imagine an old woman knocking back glasses of Calvados? But when I have company, I confess that I'm delighted at the opportunity.'

Too bad. Why not! He felt good. He was a little hot in that cramped room with the sun's rays striking his shoulder. Valentine, who had told him to sit in her chair, poured his drink, lively and alert, her eyes shining almost girlishly.

'Did Charles talk to you about anything else?'

'About what?'

'About his brother.'

'He simply told me that he didn't understand why Théo showed himself in such a bad light and said that he seemed to be doing it deliberately. He was put out. He's full of admiration for Théo and he has a very strong sense of family. I'll wager that he's not the one who spoke ill of me.'

'That's correct.'

'Who did?'

He had barely been in the house three minutes, and now he was being interrogated, almost without his realizing it.

'It was my daughter, wasn't it?'

But she said it with a smile.

'Don't be afraid of betraying her. She hasn't tried to conceal it from me. She told me that she had spoken frankly to you.'

'I don't think your daughter's very happy.'

'Do you imagine she wants to be?'

She smiled at her glass, at Maigret.

'I don't know if you've spent a lot of time with women. Young Rose, for example, would have been terribly unhappy if she hadn't been continuously pondering questions – philosophical questions, you understand – which she'd suddenly begin to think about, looking obstinate, barely answering me when I spoke to her, making a great racket when she was doing the washing-up, as if she were being prevented from finding a solution on which the fate of the world depended.'

'Is it true that she no longer visited her parents?'

'She seldom went because each time there was a row.'

'Why?'

'Can't you guess? She'd arrive there with her all-important questions, giving them advice based on the latest books she'd read, and naturally they said she was a silly fool.'

'She didn't have any friends?'

'For the same reason. And for the same reason again she

didn't go out with the local boys, who were too coarse and down-to-earth for her liking.'

'So, apart from you, she spoke to virtually no one?'

'She did the shopping, but she can't have opened her mouth much. I'm sorry! I was forgetting the doctor. On my shelves Rose found a book on medicine which she dipped into from time to time, after which she asked me questions I couldn't answer:

'"Admit you know I haven't got long to live?"

'"Are you ill, Rose?"

'She'd think she'd just discovered that she had a cancer, or better still, a rare disease. It would worry her for a few days, and then she'd ask me for an hour off to rush to the doctor's.

'Perhaps it was also a chance for her to talk about her problems, because Jolly listened to her patiently, without laughing, without ever contradicting her.'

'Did she spend her evenings with you?'

'I never saw her in the sitting room and, besides, I shouldn't have liked that. Do you find me old-fashioned? As soon as she'd finished her washing-up, she'd go upstairs to her room and, without getting undressed, would lie down on her bed with a book and smoke cigarettes. She certainly didn't like the taste of tobacco. She didn't know how to smoke. She'd have to keep closing her eyes, but that was her idea of poetry. Am I cruel? Not as cruel as you think. When I went upstairs, she'd appear, her face flushed, her eyes shining, and she'd wait until I was in bed before giving me my medicine.

'"Don't forget to air your room before going to bed."

Those were my ritual words, because of the cigarette smoke that seeped under the doors. And she'd reply:

'"No, madame. Good night, madame."

'Then she'd make as much noise getting undressed as an entire roomful of girls.'

Madame Leroy was also making a racket in the kitchen, but it was as if she was doing it for the sake of it, to assert her independence. She came to the door with a surly expression, gazing at Maigret blankly as if he weren't there.

'Shall I put the soup on?'

'Don't forget the marrow bone.'

And turning towards Maigret, Valentine continued:

'In short, apart from my son-in-law Julien you've met the whole family. They're not especially impressive, but they're not especially bad either, are they?'

He tried, unsuccessfully, to remember the words Arlette had used to describe her mother.

'I shall end up believing, like dear Charles, that it was all simply an inexplicable accident. You can see that I'm still alive and that if someone did decide at some point they wanted to kill me – God knows why – they would appear to have given up. What do you think?'

He didn't think at all. He watched her, his eyes a little hazy, the sunlight dancing between them. A vague smile hovered on his lips – Madame Maigret would have said that he was blissful – as he wondered, without detracting from the tragedy of the situation, as though in a game, if it was possible to disconcert such a woman.

He took his time, letting her talk, occasionally raising

his glass of Calvados to his lips, and the fruity aroma of the alcohol became for him the smell of the house, mingled with the cooking aromas, a hint of wax floor polish and 'cleanliness'.

She probably didn't rely on the maids to do the cleaning, and he pictured her in the mornings, a cap on her head, dusting the numerous fragile knick-knacks herself.

'You find me eccentric? Are you going to come to the conclusion, like some people around here, that I'm a mad old woman? You'll see one of these days! When you get old, you don't care what people think about you any more, and you do as you please.'

'Have you seen Théo again?'

'No. Why?'

'Do you know which hotel he's staying at?'

'I think I heard him say on Sunday that he had a room at the Hôtel des Anglais.'

'No. He's at the Hôtel de la Plage.'

'Why do you think he'd have come back to see me?'

'I don't know. He knew young Rose well.'

'Théo?'

'He went out with her a few times.'

'It can't have been often, because she hardly ever left the house.'

'Did you stop her?'

'Naturally I didn't allow her to run around the streets at night.'

'But she did. How many days off did she have?'

'Two Sundays per month. She would leave after doing the washing-up from lunch, and when she went to visit her parents she wouldn't come back until the Monday morning, on the first bus.'

'So you'd be alone in the house?'

'I've already told you that I'm not afraid. Are you saying there was something going on between her and Théo?'

'He says she was content just to talk to him about her problems.'

And he added a little disloyally:

'. . . holding his hand or resting her head on his shoulder!'

She laughed. She laughed so heartily that she became breathless.

'Quick, tell me it's not true.'

'It's the absolute truth. It's even the reason why Charles isn't very proud of his brother at the moment.'

'Did Théo talk to you about it in front of him?'

'He had to. He realized I knew.'

'And how did you know?'

'First of all because I ran into him yesterday in the company of Rose's brother.'

'Henri?'

'Yes. They were deep in conversation in a café in town.'

'How do they know one another?'

'I have no idea. He says that Henri was also aware of the relationship and came to see him to ask for an explanation.'

'It's too funny! If I hadn't heard it from you . . . You see, Monsieur Maigret, you have to know Théo to appreciate the flavour of what you're telling me. He's the biggest snob on earth. It's become almost his sole raison d'être.

He would happily be bored to death anywhere so long as it was somewhere exclusive, and he'd travel hundreds of kilometres to be seen in the company of someone dazzling.'

'I know.'

'The idea of him walking hand in hand with young Rose . . . Listen! There's one thing about my maid you don't know, and that probably no one has thought to tell you. It's a pity her parents took away her things. I'd have shown you her wardrobe, especially her hats. Think of the most outlandish colours, colours that clash with each other. Rose had a very big bosom. Now when she went out, she'd wear clothes that were so tight-fitting she could scarcely breathe. I'd never have allowed her to dress like that here. And on those days, she'd avoid me on her way out and on her return because her make-up was so excessive, so clumsily applied, that she looked like one of those girls that you see on certain street corners in Paris. Théo and her. Heavens!'

And she laughed again, more nervously.

'Tell me, where did they go?'

'I only know that they met at the Vaucottes fair and that they sometimes had a drink in a little café in Étretat.'

'How long ago?'

He seemed half asleep now. A faint smile on his lips, he watched her through his eyelashes.

'As recently as last Wednesday.'

'Did Théo admit it to you?'

'Not willingly, but he admitted it nevertheless.'

'Now I've seen everything. I hope at least that he didn't

come and visit her in my house, like my daughter's lover, by climbing in through the window.'

'He says he didn't.'

'Théo . . .' she repeated, still incredulous.

Then she got up to refill their glasses.

'I can see Henri, the hard man of the family, coming to demand an explanation! But—'

Her expression changed from ironic to serious, and then she looked amused.

'That would take the biscuit . . . It's two months, isn't it, that Théo's been in Étretat . . . Supposing . . . No! It's too outlandish . . .'

'Do you think he could've made her pregnant?'

'No! Forgive me. It did occur to me but . . . Did it cross your mind too?'

'Briefly.'

'That still wouldn't explain anything.'

The gardener appeared on the other side of the glazed door, and waited without moving, certain that they would eventually notice him.

'Would you excuse me for a moment? I have to go and give him instructions.'

Ah! There was the tick-tock of a clock which he hadn't noticed until now, and he eventually identified the regular noise coming from upstairs: it was the purring of the cat, most likely lying on its mistress's bed, that could be heard through the thin ceiling of this doll's house.

The sun, broken up into tiny squares by the window-panes, danced on the knick-knacks, creating reflections and outlining the very clear shape of a linden leaf on the varnished tabletop. In the kitchen Madame Leroy was making such a din that it sounded as if she was moving furniture around. The scratching in the garden resumed.

Maigret had the impression that he hadn't stopped hearing it, but when he opened his eyes, he was surprised to see Valentine's face just a metre from his.

She smiled hastily so he wouldn't feel uncomfortable, and he muttered, his mouth furry:

'I think I dozed off.'

7. The Almanac Predictions

When it was time for Maigret to leave, he and the old lady were in such a cheerful mood that it wouldn't have been surprising to see them clapping each other on the back.

Once the door had closed, was Valentine still smiling? Or, as after some fits of uncontrollable laughter, had her mood abruptly swung when she found herself alone with the frosty Madame Leroy?

In any event, it was a worried Maigret who plodded heavily back to town, heading in the direction of Doctor Jolly's house. At one point Castaing appeared as if out of a wall, but that wall was a tavern, a strategic place where the inspector had been waiting for some time, playing cards.

'I saw the doctor, chief. There was nothing wrong with Rose. She was the picture of health. All the same, she'd go and see him from time to time and he'd prescribe her harmless medicines to keep her happy.'

'Which were . . .?'

'Hormones. She was the one who asked for them, all she could talk about was her glands.'

Baffled, Castaing fell into step beside Maigret and asked:

'Are you going back there?'

'Only one question to ask him. You can wait.'

He treated Castaing, who did not belong to his squad,

with familiarity, and it was a sign. A large, square house with ivy-covered walls came into view, surrounded by a garden that resembled a small park.

'That's his place,' said Castaing. 'But he's in the lodge, on the left, where he sees his patients.'

The lodge was like a shed. Doubtless there was a Madame Jolly who didn't like the patients and the pharmaceutical smells and had booted them all out of her home.

'Make sure he sees you when he opens the door. Otherwise you'll have to wait for hours.'

The walls were whitewashed. All around, women, children and old men were sitting on benches, waiting. There were at least twelve people.

A boy with his head swaddled in a big bandage and a woman wrapped in a shawl desperately trying to soothe a baby in her arms. All eyes were on a door at the back of the room from behind which came the murmur of voices, and Maigret was lucky enough to see that door open almost at once: a plump farm woman came out and the doctor looked around the room and spotted him.

'Do come in. Would you excuse me for a moment?'

He counted the patients, separated the wheat from the chaff in other words, and addressed three or four people, saying:

'I won't be able to see you today. Come back the day after tomorrow at the same time.'

He closed the door.

'Let's go into the house. You'll have a drink, won't you?'

'I have just one question to ask you.'

'But I'm delighted to see you and I shan't allow you to leave so fast.'

He opened a side door and led Maigret across the garden towards the big, square house.

'It's a pity that my wife's gone to Le Havre today. She would have been so thrilled to meet you!'

The interior was lavish, comfortable but slightly gloomy because of the big trees in the garden.

'The inspector came by earlier and I told him that, far from being ill, young Rose was built to live to be a hundred. I have rarely come across a family as robust as hers. You should have seen her frame.'

'Was she pregnant?'

'What kind of question is that? That's the last thing I'd have asked myself. She came to see me not long ago, and she didn't mention anything of the sort. Around three months back I gave her a complete check-up and I could almost swear that at that point she'd never had sexual intercourse. What would you like to drink?'

'Nothing. I've just come from Valentine's, where I was obliged to drink more than I'd have liked.'

'How is she? Another one who's robust and who could manage perfectly well without a doctor. A delightful woman, isn't she? I knew her before her second marriage, and even before the first. It was me who delivered her baby.'

'Do you consider her to be completely normal?'

'You mean mentally? Because she can sometimes be eccentric? Beware of those people, inspector. They're usually the ones with their heads screwed on. She knows what she's doing, all right! She always has. She loves her little life, her little house, her little comforts. Can you blame her? I have no concerns about her, I assure you!'

'What about young Rose?'

Maigret thought about the patients who were waiting, the woman cradling her baby, the boy with his bandaged head. But the doctor, who seemed in no hurry, had lit a cigar and settled into an armchair ready for a lengthy conversation.

'There are thousands of girls like young Rose in France. You know her background. She probably spent three years at most at her village school. Then she suddenly found herself in another world. People talked to her too much. She read too much. Do you know what she asked me on one of her visits? What I thought of Freud's theories. She was also worried that her glandular system was deficient, and goodness knows what else.

'I pretended to take her seriously. I let her talk. I prescribed medication that had as much effect on her as water.'

'Was she miserable?'

'Not at all. On the contrary, she was very cheerful when she allowed herself to be. Then she started thinking, as she said, and she'd take herself very seriously. She must have come across Dostoyevsky at Valentine's, and she read him from cover to cover.'

'Did any of the drugs you prescribed for her contain arsenic?'

'None, you can be assured.'

'Thank you very much.'

'Are you leaving already? I should so like to have you here for a while.'

'I'll be back, no doubt.'

'If you promise me . . .'

He sighed, irked at having to go back to work so soon.

Castaing was waiting outside.

'What are you going to do now?'

'I'm going to take a trip to Yport.'

'Shall I drive you there in the Simca?'

'No. I think you might do better to telephone your wife and tell her that you'll probably be home late, perhaps not at all.'

'She's used to it. How are you going to get there? There's no bus at this hour. You can't walk all the way.'

'I'll take a taxi.'

'If one of them is free. Because there are only two taxis in Étretat. Look! The office is on the corner of this little street. What would you like me to do in the meantime?'

'You're going to go in search of Théo Besson.'

'That won't be difficult. I simply need to do the round of all the bars. And then?'

'Nothing. Watch him.'

'Discreetly?'

'It doesn't matter if he sees you. The main thing is not to let him give you the slip. If he drives out of town, you have your car. Park close to his, which is probably at the hotel. If that happens, try to leave me a note or send a message to my hotel. I don't think he'll go far.'

'If you're going to see the Trochus, I hope you have fun.'

The sun was beginning to set when Maigret left town

in a taxi whose driver kept turning round to talk to him. Maigret always seemed to be dozing, puffing occasionally on his pipe, looking out at the countryside, which was turning a dark, dingy green, with lights coming on in the farms and cows lowing at the gates.

Yport was no more than a fishing village with a few houses that rented rooms to summer visitors, like all seaside places. The driver had to ask for directions, because he didn't know the Trochus. He pulled up in front of a single-storey house with nets drying outside.

'Shall I wait for you?'

'Please.'

A face was just visible at the window and, when Maigret knocked on the brown door, he heard the clatter of cutlery, telling him that the family was eating.

It was Henri who opened the door, his mouth full. He stared at Maigret in silence without asking him in. Behind him burned a hearth fire which lit up the room and above which hung a big cooking pot. Next to it was a stove, a magnificent, nearly new one, but it was clearly a luxury which was only used on special occasions.

'May I speak to your father?'

The father could see him too, but hadn't said a word so far. There were five or six of them sitting around a long table with no cloth, steaming plates in front of them. In the centre was a huge dish of potatoes and cod in a white sauce. The mother turned her back to the door. A fair-haired little boy twisted round to look at the interloper.

'Ask him in, Henri,' said the father at length.

And, wiping his mouth on the back of his sleeve, he rose

so slowly that the movement appeared almost solemn. He seemed to be saying to his brood: 'Don't be afraid. I'm here and nothing can happen to you.'

Henri did not resume his seat at the table but stayed standing beside an iron bed, beneath a reproduction of Millet's *Angelus*.

'I presume you're the boss of the one who was here before?'

'I am Detective Chief Inspector Maigret.'

'And what do you want from us now?'

He had a magnificent seafarer's face, much beloved of Sunday painters, and he kept his cap on even inside the house. He was as broad as he was tall, in his blue jumper that made his chest look even bigger.

'I'm trying to find out who killed—'

'My daughter!' broke in Trochu, intent on pointing out that it was his daughter and no one else who was dead.

'Exactly. I'm sorry for having to disturb you. I wasn't expecting to find you at supper.'

'What time do you people eat? Later, of course, like everyone else who doesn't have to get up at four thirty in the morning.'

'Do please carry on with your meal.'

'I've finished.'

The others continued eating in silence with awkward movements, staring at Maigret and taking in every word their father said. Henri had lit a cigarette, perhaps as a gesture of defiance. No one had offered a chair to Maigret, who seemed huge standing in the low-ceilinged room with sausages dangling from the beams.

There wasn't just one bed in the room but two, one of them a child's cot, and an open door revealed a bedroom with three more, but no washstand, which suggested that they all had to wash outside at the well.

'You brought back all your daughter's belongings?'

'I'm entitled to, aren't I?'

'That's not a criticism. It might help me in my investigation to know exactly what they consisted of.'

Trochu turned to his wife, whose face Maigret finally saw. She looked young to have such a large family, including grown-up children like Rose and Henri. She was thin and dressed in black, with a medallion around her neck.

They looked at each other in confusion and the children fidgeted on their bench.

'We've already shared them out.'

'Are some of the items not here any more?'

'Jeanne, who works in Le Havre, took the dresses and linen that fitted her. She couldn't take the shoes because they were too small.'

'I've got them!' said a girl of around fourteen, with fat auburn plaits.

'Shut up!'

'I'm not so much interested in the clothes but in the small items. Were there any letters?'

This time the parents turned to look at Henri, who seemed disinclined to reply. Maigret repeated his question.

'No,' he snapped.

'No diary either, no notes?'

'I only found the almanac.'

'What almanac?'

He went to fetch it from the bedroom next door. Maigret remembered that, when he was young and lived in the country, he had seen those almanacs, shoddily printed on cheap paper, with naive illustrations. He was surprised they still existed.

Each day of the month was followed by a prediction. For example:

17 August. Melancholy.
18 August. Do not undertake anything. Do not travel.
19 August. The morning will be cheerful, but beware of the evening.

He did not smile as he solemnly flicked through the well-thumbed little book. But he found nothing special in September, or at the end of the previous month.

'You didn't find any other papers?'

Then the mother too stood up and spoke and Maigret could sense that the entire family was with her, applauding the reply they'd been hoping for.

'Do you really think it's right for you to come here asking these questions? I'd like to be told once and for all whether it's my daughter who's dead, yes or no. And if she is, then it's not us you should come bothering but those people, the ones you're making sure to leave in peace.'

There was a tangible feeling of relief in the air. The fourteen-year-old looked as if she was about to start clapping.

'Because we're poor,' she went on, 'because some people put on airs and graces—'

'I can assure you, madame, that I question rich and poor alike.'

'What about those who act rich when they're not? What about those who act high and mighty and are from a lower class than us?'

Maigret didn't bat an eyelid, hoping that she would continue, and she did, after looking about her to pluck up the courage.

'Do you know who that woman is? Well let me tell you. When my poor mother got married, she married a good boy who had been in love with another woman for a long time, Valentine's mother that was, and the two of them lived almost next door to one another. Well! The boy's parents never wanted him to marry her. That's telling you what sort of girl she was . . .'

If Maigret understood correctly, it was Valentine's mother who was the sort of girl men didn't wed.

'She got married, you'll tell me, but she only managed to find a drunkard, a good-for-nothing, and it was from those two that Madame was born!'

Trochu, the father, had taken a short pipe from his pocket and was filling it in a tobacco pouch made from a pig's bladder.

'I was against my daughter working for a woman like that, who was possibly worse than her mother. If they'd listened to me—'

A glance full of reproach at her husband's back. He must have given Rose permission to enter into Valentine's service.

'On top of that, she's a nasty piece of work. Don't laugh.

I know what I'm talking about. She probably took you in with her false airs. But believe you me, she's a nasty piece of work – she envies everyone, she's always hated my Rose.'

'Why did your daughter stay with her?'

'I still wonder. Because she didn't like her either.'

'Did she tell you so?'

'She didn't tell me anything. She never talked about her employers. In the end, she hardly talked to us at all any more. We weren't good enough for her, you see. That's what that woman did. She taught her to despise her parents, and that I'll never forgive her. Now Rose is dead, and that woman came and put on her airs and graces at her funeral, whereas her rightful place is probably in prison!'

Her husband gave her a look as if to try to pacify her.

'At any rate, you don't need to come poking around here!' she concluded vehemently.

'May I say something?'

'Let him speak,' said Henri.

'We policemen aren't magicians. How can we find out who committed a crime if we don't know why the crime has been committed?'

He spoke softly, kindly.

'Your daughter was poisoned. By whom? I'll know the answer probably when I find out *why* she was poisoned.'

'That woman hated her, I tell you.'

'That might not be reason enough. Murder is a very serious act, remember, where you risk your own skin, and in any case your freedom.'

'Evil people don't risk much.'

'I think your son will know what I mean when I say that there were others who were close to Rose.'

Henri looked uncomfortable.

'And there are perhaps others still, whom we don't know. That's why I hoped to examine her belongings. There might have been letters, addresses, even objects that were given to her as presents.'

At the mention of presents there was a silence and glances were exchanged. They seemed to be questioning one another and finally the mother said, with a last trace of wariness:

'Are you going to show him the ring?'

She was speaking to her husband, who decided, as if reluctantly, to extract a large, worn wallet from his trouser pocket. It had a number of compartments, one of which closed with a press stud. He took out an object wrapped in tissue paper which he held out to Maigret. It was an antique-style ring, set with a green stone.

'I presume your daughter had other jewellery?'

'There was a little box – full of things she'd bought herself at the fairs in Fécamp. They've already been shared out. There are still some here.'

The girl, without saying anything, ran into the bedroom and came back with a silver bracelet decorated with blue porcelain stones.

'This is my share!' she said proudly.

None of it was worth very much – rings, medals, mementos of her first communion.

'Was this ring with the other things?'

'No.'

The fisherman turned to his wife, who was still slightly undecided.

'I found it in the toe of a shoe, inside a little ball of tissue paper. They were her Sunday shoes, she'd only worn them a couple of times.'

The glow from the fire didn't provide enough light to examine the ring, and Maigret was no expert in precious stones, but it was obvious that this jewel was of a different quality from the other items they had mentioned.

'I'll say it,' blurted out Trochu at last, his face red. 'That thing bothered me. Yesterday I went to Fécamp, so I took the opportunity to go and see the jeweller where we bought our wedding rings. I wrote down the word he said on a piece of paper. It was an emerald. He also said it was worth as much as a boat and that if I had found it I should take it to the police.'

Maigret turned to Henri.

'Is it because of that?' he asked him.

Henri nodded.

The mother asked suspiciously:

'What are you two up to? Have you met before?'

'I think it's best to tell you. I saw your son in the company of Théo Besson. I was surprised, but now I understand. The fact is that Théo went out with Rose a couple of times.'

'Is that true?' she asked Henri.

'It's true.'

'You knew? And you didn't say anything?'

'I went and asked him if he was the person who had given my sister a ring and what exactly was going on between them.'

'What did he say?'

'He asked to see the ring. I couldn't show it to him, because father had it in his pocket. I described it to him. I didn't know then that it was an emerald, but he immediately said that word.'

'Was it him?'

'No. He swore he'd never given her any presents. He explained that they were just friends and that he enjoyed talking to her because she was clever.'

'Did you believe him? Do you believe anything said by a member of that family?'

Henri looked at Maigret and went on:

'He's also trying to find out the truth. He claims that it's not the police who'll get to the bottom of it. He even says' – and his lips trembled a little – 'that it was Valentine who brought you here and that it's as if you were in her employ.'

'I am not in anyone's employ.'

'I'm repeating what he said.'

'Are you certain, Henri, that it wasn't Théo who gave your sister the ring?' asked the father, embarrassed.

'He seemed to me to be telling the truth. He also said that he wasn't rich and that even if he sold his motor car, he wouldn't be able to afford a ring like that, assuming that the stone is genuine.'

'Where does he think it comes from?' asked Maigret.

'He doesn't know either.'

'Did Rose ever go to Paris?'

'She never set foot there in her life.'

'Me neither,' broke in the mother. 'And I have no wish

to go there. It's bad enough having to go to Le Havre from time to time.'

'Did she go to Le Havre?'

'She'd sometimes go and visit her sister.'

'To Dieppe too?'

'I don't think so. What would she go to Dieppe for?'

'The truth is,' said Madame Trochu, 'that these last months we knew almost nothing about her. When she came to see us, it was a flying visit, to criticize everything we did, everything we said. If she did open her mouth, she didn't talk the way we taught her, but used words that we couldn't understand.'

'Was she fond of Valentine?'

'You mean did she like her? My feeling is that she hated her. I gathered that from a few things she said.'

'Such as?'

'I can't recall right now, but it struck me at the time.'

'Why did she carry on working for her?'

'That's what I often used to ask her. She wouldn't answer.'

Trochu then made the gesture that Inspector Castaing had told him would come at the last minute.

'We haven't offered you a drink. Will you have a glass of cider? Since you haven't eaten, I won't offer you spirits.'

He went outside to draw the cider from the barrel in the shed and came back with a full bluish stoneware pitcher. Then he took a cloth out of a drawer to wipe two glasses.

'Would you entrust the ring to me for a couple of days?'

'It's not ours. I don't think it ever belonged to my daughter. If you take it away, you must give me a receipt.'

Maigret wrote one out on the corner of the table, which they cleared to give him room. He drank the cider, which was a little young, but he praised it effusively, because Trochu brewed it himself every autumn.

'Believe me,' said the mother, showing him to the door. 'It was definitely Rose the killer was after. And if anyone tries to tell you otherwise, it's because they have good reason to.'

'I hope we'll soon find out.'

'Do you think it'll be that fast?'

'Perhaps faster than you think.'

He had pushed the ring wrapped in tissue paper into his waistcoat pocket. He looked at the folding cot which must have been Rose's when she was little, the bedroom where she had slept when she was older with her sisters, the fireplace in front of which she would have crouched to make the soup.

While he wasn't exactly an enemy, he was an outsider and the family were still wary as they watched him leave. Only Henri walked Maigret to his taxi.

'Would you mind giving me a lift to Étretat?'

'I'd be delighted.'

'I'll just go and get my cap and my bag.'

Maigret heard Henri explaining to his family:

'I'm getting a lift from the inspector. From Étretat I'll go straight to Fécamp to set sail.'

He returned with a sailcloth bag which must have contained his fishing equipment. The car pulled away. Maigret looked over his shoulder and saw the family silhouetted in the open doorway.

'Do you think he lied to me?' asked Henri, lighting a cigarette.

His clothes gave off a strong smell of brine.

'I don't know.'

'Are you going to show him the ring?'

'Maybe.'

'When I went to find him the first time, I wanted to beat him up.'

'So I gathered. What I'm wondering is, how did he go about winning you over.'

Henri began to think.

'I'm wondering the same thing. He's not how I imagined him, and I'm convinced he didn't try to sleep with my sister.'

'Did others try?'

'The Babœuf boy, when she was seventeen, and you can be sure he didn't get anywhere.'

'Did Rose ever talk of getting married?'

'Who to?'

He too must have had the feeling that there was no one suitable in the area for his sister.

'Is there something you wanted to tell me?'

'No.'

'Why did you come with me?'

'I don't know. I want to see him again.'

'To ask him about the ring once more?'

'About that and everything else. I'm not educated like you, but I get the feeling there's something unnatural.'

'Are you hoping to find him in the little bar where I saw the pair of you?'

'There or elsewhere. But I'd rather you dropped me before.'

He got out as they entered the town and sauntered off, his bag slung over his shoulder, after a mumbled thank you.

Maigret dropped into his hotel first, where he found no message waiting for him, and then he pushed open the door of Charlie's bar, at the casino.

'Have you seen my inspector?'

'He was here before dinner.'

Charlie looked at the clock, which showed nine, and added:

'That was a while ago.'

'Théo Besson?'

'They came in and left more or less at the same time.'

He winked to show he had understood.

'Aren't you having anything?'

'No thank you.'

It looked as if Henri had made the trip to Étretat for nothing, because Maigret found Castaing watching the Hôtel de la Plage.

'Is he in there?'

'He went up to his room a quarter of an hour ago.'

Castaing pointed to a light at a second-floor window.

8. *The Light in the Garden*

Two or three times that evening Castaing gave Maigret a sidelong glance, wondering whether he knew where he was going, whether he really was the great detective that young police officers tried to emulate or whether, today at any rate, he wasn't wasting everyone's time, or at least allowing himself to be led by events.

'Let's sit down for a moment,' said Maigret when he joined Castaing across the road from the hotel he was watching.

The upstanding citizens who protest against the number of bars are unaware that they are a godsend for the police. As if by chance, there was one fifty metres from the Hôtel de la Plage and, by craning their necks, they could watch Théo's window from their table.

Castaing had thought that Maigret wanted to speak to him, to give him instructions.

'I fancy a shot of Calvados in my coffee,' confessed Maigret. 'It's not very warm this evening.'

'Have you eaten?'

'I haven't, as a matter of fact.'

'Aren't you going to?'

'Not now.'

But he wasn't drunk. He must have consumed a lot of alcohol during the day, here and there, and that was probably why he seemed so leaden.

'He might be going to bed,' he remarked, looking at the window.

'Shall I carry on watching the place?'

'You carry on, son. So long as you don't take your eyes off the hotel entrance, which is more important than the window, you can stay here. Meanwhile, I think I'll drop into Valentine's to say good night.'

But he sat there for a good fifteen minutes more, in silence, staring vacantly in front of him. Finally he got up, sighing, and left, his pipe in his mouth, his hands in his pockets, heading off into the empty streets; Castaing heard his footsteps fade.

It was a few minutes before ten when Maigret reached the gate of La Bicoque, on the road lit by a crescent moon surrounded by a dense halo. He hadn't met a soul on the way. Not a dog had barked, no cat had leaped into a hedge as he passed. The only sound was the regular croaking of the frogs in some pond.

Raising himself up on to his tiptoes, he tried to see if there was still a light on in the old lady's house, thought he saw one on the ground floor and walked through the open gate.

It was damp in the garden, and there was a powerful smell of compost. He had difficulty following the path without getting caught on some of the branches, and the rustling of the foliage must have been audible inside the house.

He reached the paved area close to it, saw the sitting room with the lights on and, there, Valentine, who rose from her armchair, straining to listen. She stood still for a moment before going over to the wall and, just when he least expected it, turning off the light.

Just then, he sneezed. A creaking sound told him that one of the windows was being opened.

'Who's there?'

'It's me, Maigret.'

A little laugh, not without a hint of nervousness, like that of someone who nonetheless had been scared.

'I'm sorry. I'll put the light on again straight away.'

And, softly, as if to herself:

'The stupid thing is, I can't find the switch. Ah! Here it is.'

She must have pushed two, because not only did the light come back on in the living room, but another one came on in the garden, almost above Maigret's head.

'I'll come and open the door.'

She was dressed as usual and, on a pedestal table in front of the armchair where he had caught her unawares, a deck of playing cards was spread out for a game of patience.

She worked her way slowly through the empty house, going from room to room, turning keys, drawing bolts.

'You see I'm not as brave as I claim and I'm barricading myself in. I wasn't expecting you.'

She didn't want to ask him any questions, but she was intrigued.

'Do you have a minute? Come in and sit down.'

And seeing him glance at the cards:

'You have to entertain yourself when you're on your own. What would you like to drink?'

'Do you know that since I've been in Étretat I've been

drinking all day long? Your stepson Charles arrives in the morning and has me drink picon-grenadines. Théo joins us and buys a round. When I meet Inspector Castaing, we go into a bar for a chat. I come here and the bottle of Calvados automatically appears on the table. The doctor is no less hospitable. The Trochus serve me cider.'

'Were they friendly?'

'Not too bad.'

'Did they tell you anything helpful?'

'Possibly. At this stage it's hard to tell what's helpful and what isn't. Has anyone been to see you since I left?'

'No one. But I paid a visit. I went to say hello to the elderly Seuret sister. She is so old that everyone thinks she's dead and no one goes to see her any more. She's my close neighbour. I could just hop over the hedge if I were still young enough.

'You see. Now I'm alone. My dragon left ages ago. I was intending to hire a new girl who would live in, but I'm not sure that I will, I so enjoy being on my own.'

'Aren't you afraid?'

'Sometimes, as you saw. Earlier, when I heard your footsteps, I slightly lost my nerve. I wondered what I'd do if I had a visit from a prowler. You tell me if this is a good plan. First of all, switch off the light in the house and then switch on the one outside, so as to see without being seen.'

'That sounds like an excellent plan to me.'

'The thing is that earlier I forgot to switch the outside light on. I must try and remember next time and be able to find the switch.'

He looked at her feet and noticed that she was wearing shoes rather than slippers. But would she permit herself to wear slippers, even in her own house, anywhere other than in her bedroom?

'Still nothing to report, Monsieur Maigret?'

He was sitting in what had already almost become his armchair, and the room was even cosier at night than during the day, with its circles of soft light beneath the lamps and large areas of shadow. The cat was downstairs, on one of the armchairs, and it soon came over to rub itself against Maigret's leg, its tail raised.

'You don't understand cat language, do you?' she joked.

'No. Why?'

'Because he's asking you to stroke him. Were you worried about me?'

'I wanted to reassure myself that all was well.'

'Are you reassured? Tell me! I hope you're not making some poor police officer spend the night out on the road to protect me? If you are, you must tell me and I'll set up a camp bed for him in the kitchen.'

She was very cheerful, with a little twinkle in her eyes. She had brought in the bottle and poured herself a glass as full as Maigret's.

'Does your wife complain about your job?'

'She's used to it by now.'

Numb in his armchair, he had filled a pipe and could see the time on a bronze clock flanked by chubby cupids.

'Do you play a lot of patience?'

'There aren't many card games for one, you know.'

'Did young Rose play?'

'I tried to teach her belote, but I never managed it.'

She must be wondering why he'd come. Perhaps, at one point, he seemed so lacklustre that she must have been afraid that he would doze off in his chair, as he had done that afternoon.

'I'd better go back to my hotel and my bed,' he sighed.

'One last drink?'

'Will you have one with me?'

'Yes.'

'Very well. I know the way now and am in no danger of getting lost. I presume you're also about to go to bed?'

'In half an hour.'

'Sleeping draught?'

'No. I didn't buy any. I'm a little afraid now.'

'Are you still able to get to sleep?'

'I nod off eventually. Elderly people don't need a lot of sleep.'

'See you tomorrow.'

'See you tomorrow.'

Again he caused a few twigs to snap and the gate creaked slightly. He stood by the roadside for a moment, looking at the edge of the roof and the chimney that rose out of the greenery in the pale moonlight.

Then he turned up the collar of his jacket against the cold damp and strode in the direction of the town.

He did the round of the town's bars that were still open, not to go in but purely to have a quick check. He was surprised not to see Henri, who must still have been trying to find Théo.

Did Henri know that he'd returned to his hotel? Had he gone there to see him?

Maybe he had set off again disappointed? Maigret didn't know what time his boat sailed from Fécamp for two weeks' fishing in the North Sea.

He went into the casino bar, which was empty, and Charlie was cashing up.

'Have you seen a fisherman?'

'The Trochu boy? He came in at least an hour ago. He was already four sheets to the wind.'

'Did he say anything?'

'Not to me. He was talking to himself. He almost forgot his bag and then, as he slung it over his shoulder, he swept the bar with it and broke two glasses.'

Castaing was outside again, probably to keep himself awake, and the light was still on in Théo's room.

'Did you bump into Rose's brother, chief? He came lurching past earlier.'

'Did he go into the hotel?'

'I don't even know whether he noticed there was a hotel.'

'Did he speak to you?'

'I pressed myself against the wall.'

'Which way was he heading?'

'He was going down the street, then he turned right, probably so as not to have to step off the pavement. What do we do?'

'Nothing.'

'Do we stay here?'

'Why not?'

'Do you think he'll come out?'

'I don't know. It's possible.'

Then, for the second time, Castaing wondered whether Maigret's reputation wasn't overrated. In any case, he shouldn't drink.

'Go and find out from the hotel if anyone came to ask for him and if anyone went up to his room.'

Castaing came back a few moments later with a negative reply.

'Are you certain that while you were following him from bar to bar he didn't speak to anyone?'

'Only to order a drink. He knew I was tailing him. He looked at me from time to time with an air of uncertainty. I think he was wondering whether it might not be easier for us to drink together.'

'Did anyone give him a letter?'

'I didn't see anything of the sort. Don't you think you'd better go and have a sandwich?'

Maigret appeared not to hear, took a cold pipe out of his pocket and slowly filled it. The halo around the crescent moon was growing denser and a thick mist was rolling in from the sea and gradually invading the streets.

It wasn't a proper fog yet, because the siren wasn't wailing.

'In a week's time,' said Castaing, 'there'll be no one left but the locals. The hotel staff will go down to the south to start a new season, with new customers.'

'What time do you make it?'

'Twenty to eleven.'

Something must have been niggling Maigret, who said, after a long pause:

'I have to leave you for a minute. I'm going to my hotel to make a telephone call.'

He made it from the booth, and called Charles Besson's home in Fécamp.

'Maigret here. I'm sorry to disturb you. I hope you hadn't gone to bed?'

'No. Have you any news? Now my wife has caught bronchitis but wants to go to the funeral tomorrow all the same.'

'Tell me, Monsieur Besson, did your wife ever own a ring set with a large emerald?'

'A what?'

He repeated his question.

'No.'

'And you've never seen such a ring in your entourage? Arlette, for example?'

'I don't think so!'

'Thank you very much.'

'Hello! Monsieur Maigret—'

'Yes.'

'What's this ring business? Have you found one?'

'I don't know yet. I'll tell you about it one of these days.'

'Is everything all right over there?'

'Everything's quiet at the moment.'

Maigret hung up, hesitated, and ended up asking for Arlette's number, in Paris. He got through immediately, faster than the previous call. A man's voice answered, and this was his first contact with Julien.

'Julien Sudre speaking,' said the calm, deep voice. 'Who's calling?'

'Detective Chief Inspector Maigret. I'd like to have a word with Madame Sudre.'

He heard him say, unruffled:

'It's for you. The inspector.'

'Hello! Is there any news?'

'I don't think so. Not yet. I'd simply like to ask you a question. Have you ever had any jewellery stolen?'

'Why are you asking me that?'

'Answer me.'

'No. I don't think so.'

'Do you have a lot?'

'Some. It was given to me by my husband.'

'Have you ever owned a ring set with a large emerald?'

There was a brief silence.

'No.'

'You don't recall a ring like that?'

'I don't, no.'

'Thank you very much.'

'Don't you have anything else to tell me?'

'Nothing tonight.'

She didn't want him to hang up. He could sense that she would have liked him to carry on talking. Perhaps she would like to have said something as well, but couldn't in front of her husband.

'Nothing unpleasant?' she merely asked.

'Nothing. Good night. I presume you were both about to go to bed?'

She thought she detected a note of sarcasm and snapped:

'Yes. Good night.'

There was no one but the night porter in the hotel lobby.

At the very end was the armchair where he had found Arlette waiting for him on the first evening. At that point he hadn't known her yet. He hadn't known anyone yet.

He wished he'd brought his overcoat, nearly telephoned Madame Maigret to say good night, shrugged and went out to join Castaing, who was still watching Théo's hotel with a glum expression. In that hotel too the lobby was empty. Nearly all the windows were dark, with the exception of two or three, and another light went off, but not the one in Théo's room.

'I wonder what he can be doing,' muttered Castaing. 'He's probably reading in bed. Unless he's fallen asleep and forgotten to switch off the light.'

'What's the time?'

'Midnight.'

'Are you certain that no one—?'

And suddenly Castaing smacked his forehead, cursed and grumbled:

'What an idiot I am! I forgot to tell you—'

'What?'

'No one spoke to him, it's true. Nor did anyone give him a letter. But, while we were in the Bar de la Poste, the second he walked in, the owner called to him:

'"Telephone call for you."'

'What time was that?'

'Just after eight o'clock.'

'He didn't say who was calling?'

'No. He went into the booth. I watched him through the glass. He wasn't doing the talking. He was listening, occasionally saying: "Yes . . . Yes . . ."'

'Is that all?'

'How on earth I could have forgotten. I hope it's not serious, chief?'

'We'll find out. How did he look as he came out of the booth?'

'I couldn't say exactly. Perhaps a little surprised? Perhaps intrigued? But not angry.'

'Come. Wait for me in the lobby.'

He asked the porter:

'Monsieur Besson's room?'

'Number 29, on the second floor. I think he's asleep. He asked not to be disturbed.'

Maigret walked past without offering any explanation. He made his way up the stairs, pausing to catch his breath, and was soon outside the white door with 29 on it in brass numbers. He knocked and there was no reply. He knocked harder, for a long time, and leaned over the banister.

'Castaing?'

'Yes, chief.'

'Ask for a master key. They must have a tool that opens all the doors.'

That took a while. Maigret emptied his pipe on to the carpet, just next to a large earthenware pot filled with sand and cigarette stubs.

The porter walked in front, disgruntled.

'As you wish! You can explain yourselves to the boss in the morning. Police or no police, this is no way to behave.'

He selected a key from a bunch hanging from a chain, but before opening he knocked discreetly and pressed his ear to the door.

They finally saw the room, which was empty, and the bed had not been slept in. Maigret opened a wardrobe to find a navy blue suit, black shoes and a gabardine. A razor and toothbrush were in the bathroom.

'The gentleman's entitled to go out, isn't he?'

'Do you know if his car's in the garage?'

'That's easy enough to find out.'

They walked back down. Instead of heading towards the main entrance, they went along a corridor, descended a few steps and Maigret noted that a little door, which wasn't locked, led directly into the garage.

The garage was completely open on to a deserted square.

'It's that one.'

Poor Castaing looked like a schoolboy wondering what sort of punishment awaited him for bad behaviour.

'Where are we going?'

'Where's your car?'

'Opposite the hotel.'

It was a stone's throw. Just as they were about to get in, the night porter dashed out on to the front steps.

'Monsieur Maigret! Monsieur Maigret! There's a phone call for you.'

'Who?'

'I don't know.'

'A woman?'

'It was a man's voice. He asked you to go to the old lady's house right away. He said you'd understand.'

They were there within moments. There was already a car outside the gate.

'The doctor's car,' said Castaing.

But they heard no sound of voices, even as they neared the house. All the lights were on, including in the upstairs rooms. A very calm Théo Besson opened the door to them, and Maigret looked at him in surprise.

'Who's wounded?'

His nostrils quivered. In the sitting room he detected the smell of cold gunpowder. On the pedestal table, where the cards were still spread out, there was a large army handgun.

He went into the guest room, where he heard someone moving about and almost knocked over Valentine carrying a heap of bloody towels, who stared at him as if sleepwalking.

On the bed that Arlette had slept in lay a man, his chest bare. He was still wearing his trousers and shoes. His face was blocked from view by Doctor Jolly's back as he leaned over him, but Maigret could already tell from the coarse blue fabric of his trousers.

'Dead?' he asked.

The doctor started, turned around and straightened up as if with relief.

'I did my utmost,' he sighed.

There was a hypodermic syringe on the bedside table. The doctor's bag, on the floor, was open and the contents in disarray. There was blood everywhere, and Maigret noticed afterwards that there was a trail in the sitting room and outside, in the garden.

'When Valentine telephoned me, I came running straight away, but it was already too late. The bullet had hit him in the aorta! Not even a transfusion, had we been able to perform one in time, could have saved him.'

'Was it you who called my hotel?'

'Yes, she asked me to inform you.'

She stood in the doorway, very close to them, blood on her hands, blood on her dress.

'It's dreadful,' she said. 'I had no idea what was going to happen when you came this evening. All that because I forgot to switch on the second light again, the one that lights up the garden.'

Maigret avoided looking at her and let out a sigh on catching sight of Henri Trochu's face; he too was now dead. Perhaps he was already thinking about what he was going to say to the family, about their reactions?

'I'll explain.'

'I know.'

'You can't know. I'd gone upstairs. I was in bed.'

As a matter of fact, this was the first time he had seen her unkempt. Her hair was in curlers and she had hastily slipped a dress over her night things, which were peeping out from underneath.

'I think I'd drifted off when the cat suddenly jumped off my bed. That's what woke me. I listened and heard a noise outside, like when you came earlier.'

'Where was the gun?'

'In my bedside drawer. It was my husband's. He got me into the habit of always having a gun within reach at night. I thought I'd told you.'

'No. Never mind.'

'First of all I looked out of the window, but it was too dark. I slipped on a dress and went downstairs.'

'Without turning the light on?'

'Yes. I couldn't see anything, but I could hear someone trying to open the door. I asked: "Who's there?"

'There was no answer.'

'Did you fire straight away?'

'I can't remember. I must have asked the question several times while someone was still fiddling with the lock. I shot through the window. I heard the man fall, and I stood there for a while not daring to go outside.'

'You didn't know who he was?'

'I had no idea. It was only then that it occurred to me to put the outside light on. Through the broken glass I saw a body and, nearby, a large bundle. Initially I'd thought that it was a prowler. I finally came out of the kitchen door and it was only when I went closer that I recognized Henri.'

'Was he alive?'

'I don't know. I ran over to Mademoiselle Seuret's, still holding the gun. I shouted at her to get up, that I needed to telephone right away and she eventually opened the door. I called Doctor Jolly and asked him to inform you or to pick you up on the way here.'

'What about Théo?'

'I found him on the doorstep when I got back.'

'Did you come back alone?'

'No. I waited on the road for the doctor.'

The doctor had just covered the dead man's face with a fold of the sheet and was making his way to the bathroom, holding his bloody hands out in front of him.

Maigret and Valentine were alone beside the body in the tiny room where they couldn't move, and Maigret still had his pipe in his mouth.

'What did Théo say to you?'

'I can't remember. He didn't say anything.'

'Weren't you surprised to see him here?'

'Probably. I don't know. Don't forget I'd just killed a man. Why do you think Henri tried to break into my house?'

He said nothing, but went into the sitting room where he found Castaing and Théo standing facing each other, both silent. Of the two, Castaing was the more anxious and he darted a desperate look at Maigret.

'It's my fault, isn't it?'

'Not necessarily.'

Théo Besson had the bored look of a man of the world caught unexpectedly in an embarrassing situation.

'You just happened to be in the vicinity, I suppose?'

He said nothing and appeared to forgive Maigret for asking him such an uncouth question.

'Come over here, you.'

He dragged Castaing outside, where he saw blood on the flagstones, the fisherman's bag lying where it had fallen.

'You're going to scoot over to his hotel. I need to know whether Théo received a telephone call during the evening. If by any chance they can't tell you, go into all the bars where Henri was hanging around.'

'They're closed.'

'Ring the bell!'

'What should I ask?'

'Whether he made a telephone call.'

Castaing didn't understand, but he was anxious to

make amends for his blunder as best he could, and he raced over to the Simca, which could soon be heard driving away.

Doctor Jolly and Valentine came down from the bathroom and the doctor's hands were white and still smelled of soap.

'I'm trying to get her to go to bed and let me give her an injection, but she won't listen. For the time being she's keeping going on nervous energy. She thinks she's strong. Fifteen minutes after I've left she'll collapse. As a matter of fact, I don't understand how she's managed to do everything she's done.'

'I killed that poor boy,' muttered Valentine, looking from Maigret to Théo, who kept to himself, silent and immobile.

'Can't you insist? She'll sleep deeply for a few hours and tomorrow she'll be on form.'

'I don't think that'll be necessary.'

Jolly frowned but bowed slightly, and looked around for his hat.

'I presume I should telephone Le Havre, like last Sunday, to ask them to remove the body? No doubt there'll be an autopsy?'

'Definitely.'

'Would you like me to pass on a message from you?'

'No thank you.'

He was about to take leave of the old lady and leaned forward as if to kiss her hand.

'You are wrong! I left a few pills in your room in case you want them. You can take one every two hours.'

He nodded in Théo's direction and went back over to Maigret, but was at a loss for words.

'I remain at your disposal of course, whenever you need me.'

He left and there was silence. When the sound of the engine faded, Valentine, as if to put on a bold front, opened the cupboard and took out the bottle of Calvados. She was about to set it down on the table when Maigret abruptly snatched it from her hands and smashed it on the floor.

'Sit down, both of you!' he said in a voice quavering with anger.

They must have obeyed him barely aware they were doing so, while he remained standing, his hands behind his back, then began to pace up and down, as he was used to doing in his office at Quai des Orfèvres.

Castaing was back already and the foghorn sent up its mournful wail into the night.

9. *Théo's Crime*

They heard Castaing turn off his engine and get out of his car, then pause on the road for a moment before opening the gate, and still Maigret said nothing. Théo, sitting in the armchair that Maigret had occupied a few hours earlier, was still trying to emulate the Duke of Windsor, while Valentine looked from one man to the other, her gaze darting rapidly between them like that of a young animal.

Castaing crossed the garden, entered the house and, taken aback by the silence and the broken bottle, wondered what to do with himself, where to put himself. Since he was not from Quai des Orfèvres, he had never seen Maigret in these circumstances.

'Well, son?'

'I got hold of the hotel owner, who was in bed, but he picked up the phone. He was the one who'd put the call through to Théo from the office – not to his room, because there are no telephones in the rooms, but to the one at the end of the corridor on his floor. It was around half past ten. The caller was drunk.'

'Have you got some paper, a pencil?'

'I have my notebook.'

'Sit down at this table. Make yourself comfortable because this will probably take a while. You are going to write down their replies.'

He started pacing again, the old lady's eyes still on him, while Théo stared at the tips of his shoes.

He eventually stopped in front of Théo, no longer angry, but he spoke with contempt.

'Were you expecting Henri to come to Étretat this evening?'

'No.'

'If he hadn't telephoned you, would you have come to La Bicoque?'

'I don't know. Possibly.'

'Where were you when he was shot? On the road? In the garden?'

'In the garden, by the gate.'

Valentine flinched on learning that she had passed close to her stepson when she had run over to old Mademoiselle Seuret's to telephone the doctor.

'Are you proud of yourself?'

'That's my business.'

'Did you know she had a gun?'

'I knew that she'd kept my father's gun. I say, inspector, would you tell me whether—'

'I'll tell you nothing at all! I'm the one who's asking the questions.'

'And supposing I refuse to answer?'

'That would make no difference whatsoever, except perhaps it would decide me to slap your face, as I've been wanting to do for the last quarter of an hour.'

Despite the tragic circumstances, despite the dead body that was still in the next room, Valentine couldn't help giving a smug, almost jolly little smile.

'How long have you known?'

'What are you talking about?'

'Look, Besson. I advise you not to be an idiot. How long have you known that your stepmother's jewellery was never sold and that she'd kept the originals and not replicas as everyone was led to believe?'

She shuddered and looked at Maigret dumbfounded, with involuntary admiration, and fidgeted in her chair as if she wanted to say something, but he took not the slightest notice of her.

'I was always convinced of it.'

'Why?'

'Because I knew her and I knew my father.'

'You mean that she was afraid of poverty and that she was not a woman not to take precautions?'

'Yes. And my father gave in to her every wish.'

'They were married under the joint-estate system?'

'Yes.'

'How much do you estimate the jewellery to be worth?'

'Probably several million at today's prices. There must be some we don't know about, because my father felt awkward to be seen spending so much money on her in front of us.'

'When he died and you were told that the jewellery had long since been sold, did you not discuss it with your brother, or with Arlette?'

'No.'

'Why not?'

'I wasn't certain.'

'Was it not rather that you planned to come to some arrangement with Valentine?'

Not a word that was said escaped Valentine, not one of Maigret's movements, not an expression of Théo's. She took in everything, much better than Castaing, whose shorthand was rudimentary.

'I shan't answer that question.'

'Which is unworthy of you, is that not so? Have you discussed it with Valentine herself?'

'Not any further.'

'Because you knew she was cleverer than you and you were waiting to have proof. How did you obtain that proof? When?'

'I asked around among my friends in the diamond world about some of the jewels which couldn't have gone unnoticed, and that's how I found out they hadn't ended up on the market, not in France, in any case, and probably not in Europe.'

'You patiently bided your time for five years.'

'I still had a little money. I pulled off a few business deals.'

'This year, finding yourself at the end of your tether, you came to spend your holidays in Étretat. It's no coincidence that you met young Rose and started to encourage her obsessions, is it?'

Silence. Valentine craned her neck, like a bird, and it was the first time that Maigret saw the wrinkled skin of her neck, which was usually concealed by a broad black velvet choker decorated with a pearl.

'Now, think before answering. When you met Rose, did

she already know or was it at your suggestion that she began nosing around the house?'

'She nosed around before meeting me.'

'Why?'

'Out of curiosity, and because she hated my stepmother.'

'Did she have reason to hate her?'

'She found her hard and proud. They lived together in this house on a war footing, so to speak, barely concealing it from one another.'

'Was it Rose who thought of the jewellery?'

'No. She drilled a hole in the partition between the two bedrooms.'

Valentine bristled, fuming, and made as if to go upstairs straight away to check whether this outrageous claim was true.

'When was that?'

'About two weeks ago, one afternoon when Valentine was having tea with Mademoiselle Seuret.'

'What did she see through the hole?'

'Nothing at first. She had to wait a few days. One night she feigned sleep, pretending to snore, then she silently got up again and saw Valentine open the chest at the foot of her bed.'

'Had Rose never looked inside?'

'All the drawers and all the cupboards in the house are locked, and Valentine keeps the keys on her. Even if she wanted a can of sardines, Rose had to ask her.'

'In that case, how did she manage to get hold of one of the rings?'

'While Valentine was having her bath. She hadn't

talked to me about it beforehand. She must have planned her move meticulously, down to the last second, so to speak.'

'Did you see the ring?'

'Yes.'

'What was she planning to do with it?'

'Nothing. She couldn't wear it without giving herself away. For her it was a sort of revenge.'

'Did you not think that your stepmother would notice?'

'Perhaps.'

'Admit that you did nothing to see what her reaction would be?'

'Possibly.'

'You would have been content to share the proceeds without saying anything to Charles and Arlette?'

'I shan't answer.'

'No doubt you're convinced that there's nothing we can do against you?'

'I haven't killed anyone.'

She bristled again, wanting to raise her hand like a schoolgirl for permission to speak.

'That's all I wanted to ask you.'

'Must I leave the room?'

'You may stay.'

'Am I free?'

'Not until further orders.'

Maigret started pacing again, slightly red in the face now that he was going to turn on the old lady.

'Did you hear?'

'Everything he says is a lie.'

Maigret took the ring out of his waistcoat pocket and showed it to her.

'Do you deny that the original jewels are in your room? Do you want me to take your keys and go and fetch them?'

'I'm perfectly entitled to them. My husband agreed. He reckoned his sons were old enough to get by on their own, and he didn't want to leave an old lady like me penniless. If the children had known, they'd have sold them and, a year later, would still have ended up broke.'

He avoided looking at her.

'Why did you hate young Rose?'

'I didn't hate her. I was suspicious of her, and events prove that I had reason to be. She was the one who had it in for me, whereas I did everything I could for her.'

'When did you discover that the ring was missing?'

She opened her mouth, nearly replied, then her expression hardened.

'I'm not going to answer any more of your questions.'

'As you wish.'

He turned to Castaing.

'Carry on taking notes.'

And, plodding heavily to and fro, making the knick-knacks tremble, he held forth:

'You probably made the discovery last week, before Wednesday. Young Rose was the only person who could have seen you and taken the ring. Most likely you searched through her things without finding anything. When she went out on Wednesday, you followed her and saw her meet Théo in Étretat.

'You began to be really afraid.

'You didn't know whether she'd talked to him about it. You suspected that it was because of the jewellery that he was here.'

Despite having resolved to say nothing, she couldn't help retorting:

'From the moment he knew, my life would have been in danger.'

'That's very possible. Mind you, I didn't ask you anything. Interrupt me if you wish, but I need no confirmation.'

'You decided to kill young Rose before she had time to betray you – or at least so you hoped – and you took advantage of a unique opportunity that presented itself. The famous 3rd of September! The only day of the year when the entire family gathers here, the family that you hate, including your daughter.'

She opened her mouth once again, but he didn't give her time to say anything.

'You knew of your maid's fascination for remedies of all sorts. You'd probably seen her stealing some from your medicine cabinet. At nights she must have been in the habit of finishing off your sleeping draught when you left some in the glass.

'You see, this crime is the crime of a woman, and of a solitary old woman at that. It's one of those carefully planned crimes, lovingly cooked up over many hours, with the constant addition of little flourishes.

'How could anyone think it was you when it seemed that you were the intended victim?

'Suspicion would inevitably fall on your daughter, or on the others.

'All you needed to do was announce that you'd found the potion bitter, that you'd said so to your servant. But I am certain you were careful not to.'

'She'd have drunk it anyway!'

She wasn't defeated, as one might have expected. She sat there, tense, without missing a word that was being said, probably planning her riposte.

'You were convinced that the investigation would be carried out by the local police, who wouldn't find anything suspicious. You only began to be afraid when you found out that Charles Besson had arranged for me to be sent from Paris.'

'You are modest, Monsieur Maigret.'

'I don't know if I am modest, but you made a mistake in coming running to Quai des Orfèvres so as to take the credit for contacting me.'

'And how, tell me, did I know that Charles had thought of you?'

'I don't know. That's a detail that will be clarified later.'

'There are a lot of details to be clarified, because you have no proof of what you are claiming with such assurance.'

Maigret ignored the challenge.

'The same goes for the jewels. Here are my keys. They are on the table in front of you. Go upstairs and look.'

He stopped pacing, looked her in the eyes, intrigued by this new problem, and appeared to be talking to himself:

'Maybe you took advantage of your trip to Paris to deposit them somewhere? No! You wouldn't have hidden them so far away. You haven't deposited them in a bank, which would have left a trail.'

She gave a mocking smile.

'Seek!'

'And I'll find.'

'If you don't find them, none of what you are saying holds water.'

'We'll come back to that when it's time.'

He bitterly regretted having smashed the bottle of Calvados in a gesture of anger, because he would gladly have had a sip.

'It's no coincidence that when I dropped by earlier to say good night to you I talked to you about the relationship between young Rose and Théo Besson, and about their meeting on Wednesday. I knew that you would react and that you'd try to see Théo out of fear that I would question him and that he'd talk, perhaps to shut him up once and for all. I wondered how you'd go about meeting him without being seen. I hadn't thought of the telephone. Or to be more precise, I hadn't thought about old Mademoiselle Seuret, who lives a stone's throw away and whom you were in the habit of visiting.'

He turned to Théo.

'Do you know her?'

'I haven't seen her for several years.'

'Is she an invalid?'

'She was already half deaf and blind back then.'

'In that case we have every chance of finding the jewellery at her house.'

'You are making the whole thing up,' she said furiously. 'You talk and talk, telling yourself that eventually you'll hit the nail on the head. And you think you're being clever!'

'You telephoned Théo from her house, and you probably called several different numbers, because it was in a bar that you finally found him. You told him you wanted to speak to him, and he understood. But you had no intention of speaking to him.

'You see, your two crimes are not only the crimes of a loner, but the crimes of an old lady.

'You are very clever, Valentine!'

She gloated, flattered by the compliment despite everything.

'Théo had to be silenced and, at the same time, you had to avoid arousing my suspicions. There was a way, which would probably have worked, but which you were loath to choose: and that was to offer to share with him.

'You are too greedy for that. The idea of losing some of your famous jewellery, which you didn't even need to live on and which has never been of any use to you, seemed so appalling that you preferred to kill a second time.

'You asked Théo to come and see you at midnight without telling anyone.

'That's what she asked you to do, isn't it, Monsieur Besson?'

'You will appreciate that it is difficult for me to answer that question. A gentleman—'

'Scoundrel! Does a gentleman involve a maid in his family affairs and incite her to commit a theft for his own ends? Does a gentleman send someone to be killed in his place?

'As a matter of fact, Monsieur Besson, after Valentine's telephone call you were both triumphant and afraid. Triumphant, because you'd won the game, because her call showed that she was ready to compromise. Afraid, because you knew her, because you realized that she wasn't exactly happy about buying your silence.

'You sensed a trap. This midnight meeting here sounded ominous.

'You went back to your hotel to think. It was a stroke of luck that poor Henri, who'd been drinking, telephoned you.

'I'd just had a conversation with him that had riled him. He began drinking and he wanted to see you, I don't know why exactly; perhaps he didn't know himself.

'So you sent him ahead as a scout, telling him to be here on the dot of midnight.

'So that he'd be the one to get caught in Valentine's trap.

'I take my hat off to you, madame. Rose's murder was admirably planned, but this one is devilishly clever.

'Right down to the trick with the light switch that you played on me this evening, which gave you the excuse to shoot in the heat of the moment without turning on the outside light.

'Except that it's Henri who's dead. The brother and the sister in the same week!

'Do you know what I'd do if I wasn't a member of the police?

'I'd leave you here under the guard of the inspector while I went to Yport to tell this story to a certain Trochu and his wife.

'I'd tell them how, why and for what sordid gain they had lost two children in the prime of life in the space of a few days.

'I'd bring them here, along with your victims' brother and sisters as well as their neighbours and friends.'

He saw Théo, who had turned ashen, grip the arm of his chair convulsively. As for Valentine, she leaped up, alarmed:

'You have no right to do that! What are you waiting for to take us to Le Havre? You have to arrest us, or arrest me in any case.'

'Do you confess?'

'I don't confess, but you're accusing me, and you don't have the right to leave me here.'

Maybe someone had already told the Trochus and they would come running.

'This is a civilized country, and everyone is entitled to a trial.'

She was straining her ears for sounds from outside and nearly threw herself against Maigret as if seeking protection when she heard the sound of a car followed by footsteps in the garden.

She was clearly on the verge of hysterics. Her face had lost its prettiness and there was panic in her eyes; her nails dug into Maigret's wrists.

'You have no right! You have no right . . .'

It wasn't the Trochus, who knew nothing yet, but the police van that had been sent from Le Havre, as well as a carful of police officers and experts.

For half an hour they took over the house. Henri's body was carried out on a stretcher while, just to be sure, an expert took photographs of the scene, including the window that the bullet had shattered.

'You may go and get dressed.'

'What about me?' asked a deflated Théo Besson, who didn't know what to do with himself.

'You, I think, need to examine your own conscience.'

Another car stopped outside on the road and Charles Besson burst into the house.

'What's happened?'

'I was expecting you earlier,' snapped Maigret.

As if not understanding what Maigret was hinting at, the politician apologized:

'I had a puncture on the way.'

'What made you come?'

'When you mentioned the ring to me over the telephone earlier.'

'I know. You recognized it from the description.'

'I realized that it was Théo who was right.'

'Because you knew that Théo suspected your stepmother of having held on to the jewellery. Had he told you?'

The two brothers glared at each other.

'He didn't say so to me, but I knew it from his behaviour when the estate was divided up.'

'You came running to claim your share? Have you even forgotten that it's your mother-in-law's funeral tomorrow morning?'

'Why are you being so harsh with me? I don't know anything. Who's just been driven off in the police van?'

'Tell me first of all why you've come here.'

'I don't know. When you mentioned the ring, I knew things would turn nasty, that Théo would try something and that Valentine wouldn't let him walk all over her.'

'Well, it's true, something did happen, but your older brother made sure to send someone else to get killed in his place.'

'Who?'

'Henri Trochu.'

'Do the parents know?'

'Not yet, and I wonder whether I shouldn't give you the task of going to inform them. After all, you're their elected representative.'

'I probably won't be any more after this scandal. What about young Rose? Who . . .?'

'Haven't you guessed?'

'When you asked me about the emerald, I thought—'

'Of your stepmother! It's her. You can explain that to your voters.'

'But *I* haven't done anything!'

For a while, Castaing, who was no longer taking notes, had been staring at Maigret, flabbergasted, while listening out for noises from the floor above.

'Are you ready?' shouted Maigret up the stairs.

And when Valentine failed to reply straight away, he read the fear on Castaing's face.

'Don't be afraid. Women like that don't kill themselves. She'll fight to the end, tooth and claw, and will find a way of hiring the best lawyers. And she knows they no longer send old women to the guillotine.'

Valentine came down, as much the grande dame as when he had seen her for the first time, with her impeccable hair and big blue eyes, her black dress without a crease and a huge diamond brooch: one of the 'replicas', of course.

'Are you going to handcuff me?'

'I'm beginning to think that you'd like that, because it would be more theatrical and would make you look like a victim. Take her away, Castaing.'

'Aren't you coming with us to Le Havre?'

'No.'

'Are you going back to Paris?'

'Tomorrow morning, after I've collected the jewellery.'

'Will you send the report?'

'You'll write it yourself. You know as much as I do.'

Castaing had lost track of what was going on.

'What about him?'

He pointed at Théo, who had just lit a cigarette and was avoiding going anywhere near his brother.

'He hasn't committed any crime as far as the law is concerned. He's too much of a coward. You'll always be able to find him when you need him.'

'Am I allowed to leave Étretat?' asked Théo with relief.

'Whenever you like.'

'Can someone drive me back to the hotel so I can pick up my car and my things?'

Like Valentine he was scared stiff of the Trochus. Maigret signalled to one of the police officers from Le Havre.

'Go with the gentleman. And by way of a farewell I give you permission to give him a kick up the backside.'

As she left La Bicoque, Valentine turned to Maigret and snarled:

'You think you're clever, but you haven't had the last word.'

When he looked at his watch, it was half past three in

the morning, and the foghorn was still wailing in the darkness. There was only one police officer from Le Havre left, who was finishing putting seals on the doors, and Charles Besson, who didn't know where to put his big body.

'I'm wondering why you were so rude to me earlier, when I haven't done anything.'

It was true, and Maigret was almost sorry.

'I swear to you that I never for one moment thought that Valentine—'

'Would you come with me?'

'Where to?'

'To Yport.'

'Do you insist?'

'It would save me having to look for a taxi, which can't be easy at this hour.'

He almost regretted it because Charles, on edge, drove erratically. He stopped the car as far as he could from the little house, which was just a dark shape in the fog.

'Do I have to wait for you?'

'Please.'

Besson, hidden from view in the darkness of the car, heard the knocks at the door and Maigret's voice saying:

'It's me, Maigret.'

Charles saw a lamp light up and the door open, and bit off the end of a cigar.

Half an hour went by, during which more than once he was tempted to drive off. Then the door opened again. Three people made their way slowly towards the car. Maigret opened the door and spoke softly:

'You will drive them to Le Havre, and you can drop me at Étretat on the way.'

From time to time the mother, wearing her veil from the funeral, stifled a sob in her handkerchief.

Meanwhile the father didn't say a word. Maigret too was silent.

When he got out of the car, in Étretat, in front of his hotel, he turned towards those sitting inside, opened his mouth, was at a loss for words and slowly raised his hat.

He did not get undressed, did not go to bed. At seven o'clock in the morning he called a taxi to take him to the old Seuret sister's house, and the same taxi dropped him at the station, in time for the eight o'clock train. In addition to his suitcases, he was carrying a little morocco leather bag whose cover was the same clear blue as Valentine's eyes.

OTHER TITLES IN THE SERIES

THE CELLARS OF THE MAJESTIC
GEORGES SIMENON

'Try to imagine a guest, a wealthy woman, staying at the Majestic with her husband, her son, a nurse and a governess... At six in the morning, she's strangled, not in her room, but in the basement locker room.'

Below stairs at a glamorous hotel on the Champs-Élysèes, the workers' lives are worlds away from the luxury enjoyed by the wealthy guests. When their worlds meet, Maigret discovers a tragic story of ambition, blackmail and unrequited love.

Translated by Howard Curtis

Other Titles in the Series

THE JUDGE'S HOUSE
GEORGES SIMENON

'He went out, lit his pipe and walked slowly to the harbour. He could hear scurrying footsteps behind him. The sea was becoming swollen. The beams of the lighthouses joined in the sky. The moon had just risen and the judge's house emerged from the darkness, all white, a crude, livid, unreal white.'

Exiled from the Police Judiciare in Paris, Maigret bides his time in a remote coastal town in France. There, among the lighthouses, mussel farms and the eerie wail of foghorns, he discovers that a community's loyalties hide unpleasant truths.

Translated by Howard Curtis

Other Titles in the Series

SIGNED, PICPUS
GEORGES SIMENON

'"It's a matter of life and death!" he said.

A small, thin man, rather dull to look at, neither young nor old, exuding the stale smell of a bachelor who does not look after himself. He pulls his fingers and cracks his knuckles while telling his tale, the way a schoolboy recites his lesson.'

A mysterious note predicting the murder of a fortune-teller; a confused old man locked in a Paris apartment; a financier who goes fishing; a South American heiress… Maigret must make his way through a frustrating maze of clues, suspects and motives to find out what connects them.

Translated by David Coward

Other Titles in the Series

INSPECTOR CADAVER
GEORGES SIMENON

'To everyone, even the old ladies hiding behind their quivering curtains, even the kids just now who had turned to stare after they had passed him, he was the intruder, the undesirable.'

Asked to help a friend in trouble, Maigret arrives in a small provincial town where curtains twitch and gossip is rife. He also finds himself facing an unexpected adversary: the pale, shifty ex-policeman they call 'Inspector Cadaver'.

Translated by William Hobson

Other Titles in the Series

FÉLICIE
GEORGES SIMENON

'In his mind's eye he would see that slim figure in the striking clothes, those wide eyes the colour of forget-me-not, the pert nose and especially the hat, that giddy, crimson bonnet perched on the top of her head with a bronze-green feather shaped like a blade stuck in it.'

Investigating the death of a retired sailor on the outskirts of Paris, Maigret meets his match in the form of the old man's housekeeper: the sharp-witted, enigmatic and elusive Félicie.

Translated by David Coward

Other Titles in the Series

Pietr the Latvian
The Late Monsieur Gallet
The Hanged Man of Saint-Pholien
The Carter of *La Providence*
The Yellow Dog
Night at the Crossroads
A Crime in Holland
The Grand Banks Café
A Man's Head
The Dancer at the Gai-Moulin
The Two-Penny Bar
The Shadow Puppet
The Saint-Fiacre Affair
Mr Hire's Engagement
The Flemish House
The Madman of Bergerac
The Misty Harbour
Liberty Bar
Lock No. 1
Maigret
Cécile is Dead
The Cellars of the Majestic
The Judge's House
Signed, Picpus
Inspector Cadaver
Félicie
Maigret Gets Angry
Maigret in New York
Maigret's Holiday
Maigret's Dead Man
Maigret's First Case
My Friend Maigret
Maigret at the Coroner's
Maigret and the Old Lady
Madame Maigret's Friend
Maigret's Memoirs
Maigret at Picratt's
And more to follow